THE LEGACY OF MANIFESTO THE GREAT

A Sci Fi Comedy Where Women Rewrite The Rules

KERRIE NOOR

CONTENTS

Glossary to do · v
Meet The Gang · vii
Preface · ix

1. The Footman's Outfit · 1
2. Meeting Mex · 6
3. Planet Hy Man's National Geographic · 10
4. The Coffee Morning · 14
5. Delegation · 19
6. Pods · 21
7. The Drawer · 25
8. Jack and John · 30
9. Winston Churchill · 34
10. The Passageway · 39
11. Legless · 44
12. The Speech · 47
13. Filing Cabinets · 51
14. Broom Closets · 58
15. Socks · 61
16. The Laboratory · 65
17. Rebellion · 69
18. Egg Cartons · 77
19. The Quarry · 83
20. Assets · 88
21. Weapons and tossing · 93
22. The Portable Intercom-Thingy · 99
23. The Beehive · 107
24. Fairy Tales · 114
25. War Cry · 119
26. The Operations Room · 127
27. The Wrong Side of the Track · 135
28. File Cabinets · 141
29. Trolleys · 146
30. The Spark Plug · 149

31. The Sandal   154
32. Knee-High   158
33. Knee-Deep   164
34. The Sailing of Socks   170
35. Polishing   175
36. Fanny's Hidden Passageway   181
    Epilogue   187

    Rebel Without A Clue—The Arrival   189
    A Note From The Author   195
    Other Books by Kerrie Noor   197

GLOSSARY TO DO

The Outlands: - a bit like the Australian outback, but with out kangaroos.

Egg Popping: an accepted profession. Eggs (also known as valuable real-estate) from a successful.

Quarry turtles: - miniature remakes of the earlier turtles; the addition of Saber—tooth teeth makes them excellent guard dogs.

Sex For Procreation Treaty:- unlike the quickly put together treatise of "your uterus - our survival" and "one shag one night," the sex for procreation treaty was an idea bandied about the spaceship by Wife-ie to give hope; no one thought that once landed it would come into force.

Bed-diving : - an act that requires neither beds nor the art of diving.

Nurturing Shed : - the tools of a nurturing shed are kept hidden from all until needed—once seen, a woman rarely opens her legs again.

The Ownership Act : - the sort of marriage most civilisations were built on.

Turtles: - the great innovation of those in the art centre, when they grew tired of transporting things, little did they know where it would lead.

MEET THE GANG

Bette: - a cleaner who has finally made it to the top.

Beryl: - a woman intent on toppling Bette.

Verruca: - Fanny's daughter, a young woman who proudly wears her name because her mother chose it——so she believes.

Mex: - a prodigy brought up to use her brain, Mex would prefer to fight, "live by the whip and die by the whip" is her motto.

Kate: - she can't help making things from biscuits to beverage makers, but will she find the one invention that "does what it says on the tin?"

Market Cleaner: - a woman as fearless as she is mouthy.

The Voted in's:- outback cleaners who rise above their station and take way too long to appreciate it.

The guru: - a man who looks like a guru until he opens his mouth.

Legless: - a footman with inspirations above his station and will happily use his body to get there.

Mr EX: - Legless's sidekick, who at one time wore trousers so tight they stopped traffic.

Fieldworkers (or celts as some like to call them):- live, breathe and die on the field farmers who want nothing more than a good yield, a good cup of hemp, and the chance to scare the living daylights out of any in the city.

Hippy's: - ex fieldworkers who moved onto better things, they couldn't care less about scaring anyone, even a mechanical mouse.

Prodigies: - the five girls Beryl plans to mold, shape, and control.

Jester and Neil: - white coats Beryl uses to mold, shape, and control her prodigies.

Big Wigs: - cleaners who rose up the ranks of power with no intention of remembering their roots.

Operators: - cleaners who not only remember their roots but try to remind others. They run the operations room a good place to be when you're in touch with your roots.

Quarry turtles: - miniature remakes of the earlier turtles; the addition of Saber—tooth teeth makes them excellent guard dogs.

Bit parts

Knee-High: - has a point to prove, mainly that size doesn't matter.

Hilda: - a cleaner who has no intention of remaining one.

Vegas:- Hilda's sidekick, she has no idea how much Hilda relies on her if she did, she would not be so intimidated by her.

PREFACE

It was Bette who decided to assign a woman to Manifesto the Great.

Somehow, sending him to the gym "didn't seem cricket," she said.

The others thought she was mad.
They had no idea what cricket was.

Chapter One

THE FOOTMAN'S OUTFIT

"A man's underwear is not something you should have to face first thing in the morning."–Bette the Cleaner

*1*945 Earth time

The day the city women took over the city was a day many tried to forget.

The city women went mad, rampaging like demented football fans —like wild dogs.

They raged in the streets, spilling into the lobby of the Building of Opulence, stopping at Hubby's statue. Realizing the pulling down of a statue was probably not a good idea, the women threw dusters instead, and when that felt good—underwear.

"Here, take that," yelled one.

"Yeah!" yelled another.

Until a woman, age undetectable, produced a spray can. Soon they were defacing on par with Fanny's "procreation graffiti."

Years of crap sex built up into the sort of crazed drawing of appendages that would have even a porn star blushing. Using every inflammatory word they could think of, they continued until the sun went down and James the Strong's massive thighs flashed onto the wall.

They stopped with breathless "where did that come from" looks;

then, realizing it was merely a Hologram, they continued with their spray-painting.

The cleaners who had stormed the room with a view moved through the corridors, finally making their way to the footman's locker room.

❖

They were heard before seen.

❖

The oaf of a footman charged into the locker room. "
They've got him," he shouted.
The footmen, mid changing, stopped.
"Who?" said one with a toss of his uniform.
"Manifesto the Great," said the oaf of a footman.
"Shit," said another.
"We're done for," screeched a voice from the shower.

❖

"He told us to save ourselves," said the oaf of a footman. "'Head for the outlands[1],' he said, 'and don't look back.'"
"A legend," muttered one.
"A hero," sighed another.
The men emptied the locker room quicker than a bomb scare. So terrified were they, they took nothing, some were still in their underpants . . .
By the time the women entered, there was nothing. Just the odd shoe, the lockers ajar and the lingering aroma of something mannish: liniment, aftershave, with a hint of shoe polish.
The smell sent the women crazy.
They stripped the lockers, tossing silk pants and jackets into the air.
"Here, kitty kitty!" they jeered, laughing like crazy as shirts and

trousers fluttered about them.

A middle-aged woman ripped off her apron, her shirt, and finally her bra.

The others stopped, silent, as the bra plopped to the ground like a pair of elephant ears.

She slid on a silk shirt with an "oooooh," stepped into a pair of trousers, and, with a wiggle, pulled the zip.

"Does my bum look big in this?" She glanced at a mirror.

The women were ecstatic; silk was as new to them as a man's groin. For years they had frumped around in aprons and itchy, floppy skirts, scrubbing things that required breath-holding.

The silk smelt of aftershave, the trousers of something unfamiliar; inhaling was as pleasant as a decent cup of tea.

Soon they were strutting about, an easy thing to do in tight silky trousers.

"This is way better than an apron," said one.

"I feel like royalty," said another.

"A new look," yelled another.

Apart, that is, from Beryl.

She appeared mid locker upturning and yelled, "What the hell is going on here!"

The women stopped, saw it was some upstart twenty something minus an apron, and carried on.

"Leave 'em," said Bette, appearing beside her. "Years of picking up after the bigwigs can do that to a girl," she said.

"Bigwigs?" said Beryl.

"Yes," said Bette, eyeing up a costume herself. "That's what we called the Readers. These girls did all their dirty work, and I mean dirty work—these men didn't lift a finger when it came to cleaning."

She looked at Beryl.

"And a man's underwear is not something you should have to face first thing in the morning."

Beryl pulled a face.

She watched as five bigwig cleaners pulled on the footmen's outfits, slid on their wigs, and charged to the back alley, yelling, "Burn —burn!"

They piled their aprons about the garbage bins and, squealing like banshees, set the pile alight.

"Burn, burn!"

They taunted as mechanical rats, squealing at the top of their lungs, raced from the bins.

The women stamped on them, reveling in their power.

"We wear the pants now," yelled one.

"Yeah, take that!" stamped another as Bette, sporting Manifesto the Great's footman's extra-tight trousers, cheered them on.

Beryl said nothing. She had no apron and drew the line at a footman's wig.

But she had her own beehive hair, and she wasn't giving that up for anything . . .

❖

Within weeks, the "bigwig" cleaners had taken over the room with a view like they took over the men.

Most of the men had been led away, stripped of their white coats, their prestige, their status, their precious caffeine. Only a few were held back to teach . . . including Jack and John.

It was all part of Bette's "transitory theory."

"If you can teach my girls, I will make it worth your while," she said. *Like they had a choice.*

Bette was at the helm, and she ruled like an overzealous born-again.

Bette, a woman whose apron betrayed her intelligence, had taken command, and with a swift tossing of her broom, she pranced about the room with a view, preaching like Billy Graham, not that anyone on Planet Hy Man knew who he was . . . yet.

Being a leader had really gone to her head.

Her first "there is more to a cleaner than disinfectant" speech went on all morning; it was longer than a Netflix serial.

"I learned many things in the shed," said Bette, "and if I can tell my egg from my spatula, so can anyone," putting a few off their morning caffeine.

"We are all pupils in life, just as we are all teachers," she said.

Some believed her, some had no idea what she was talking about, but all followed.

Bette was just so damn scary.

---

1. a bit like the Australian outback, but with out kangaroos.

Chapter Two

MEETING MEX

"After all, someone had to get their hands dirty, and it wasn't going to be her cleaners."–Bette

Every woman in the city wanted to egg pop[1]. It was considered a cushy job, the easiest on the planet; in fact, many saw it as a holiday.

It required lounging about in a room with a skylight, a mirror with a remote, and hemp on tap. One spliff, one pot of hemp tea, and a woman, glaze-eyed and chilled, laughed her way through the whole removal of her eggs. Then, as high as a nineties raver, she'd stagger into the free-of-charge, on-the-house transporter to sleep it off at home.

At first, any egg would do—until one morning, pondering by her window, Bette spied a crowd of market stall owners jostling at the entrance.

We have flooded this place with stall owners, she thought and decided genes was the only way to go.

"We need to file the eggs," she said to the committee.

"What, in a drawer?" said Bigwig One.

Bette looked at her like she was an imbecile.

"I mean store them according to whom they came from: warrior, organizer, teacher, layabout."

"Like in a filing cabinet?"

Bette threw her another look.

"And maybe give the market stall owners a rest for a while."

"But they are the cheapest. Apart from the layabouts, one spliff and they're out like a light," said the voice from the back.

The others nodded.

"Yes, well, we could probably give the layabouts a miss altogether," said Bette. "Walking down the street requires a full purse, and by the time I get to the market, I've bugger-all to spend and a sea of pissed-off stall owners staring at me."

She stopped; the committee looked at her.

"You walk down the street?"

"What do you think I do, fly?"

"But you're the leader."

Bette looked at them with a "so?"

"We always send out . . ." muttered the voice from the back, avoiding her dark look.

Beryl loved the gene theory, and while the others were trying to grasp why a leader would want to walk down a street full of minions, Beryl had planned a leaflet. After all, it was merely a reworking of Manifesto the Great's ideas.

"It's all in the labelling," she said, passing around the leaflet at the next committee meeting.

The Voted Ins, with an unimpressed sniff, eyed each other.

Beryl was such a smart-arse.

As she spoke of her plans to not only catalog the fertilized eggs but control the whole upbringing of a baby, the bigwigs, staring at her blonde beehive piled high like an ice cream sundae, argued.

Bette, saying nothing, flicked through the leaflet.

"I see you have other plans."

"Well yes, education on many levels."

"We have nans for that," jumped in Bigwig One.

"What the galaxy does a nan know?" said Beryl.

"More than that speakeasy mother of yours," snapped another.

Beryl stiffened. "Leave my mother out of this."

Bette slid the leaflet across the table. "Let's start with the nurturing, see how you get on with that."

Beryl huffed.

She was more than a nurturer, she was a planner, an order-giver, designed to lead and boss, not take orders from ex-mop welders who didn't know their arse from their eggs.

She snatched back her leaflets, shuffled them into a pocket, and marched to the door, her beehive wobbling with each step.

The women stared at the slammed door as she left. Normally they'd make fun of her hair, but this time they were silent.

"You'll regret that," said the posh bigwig. "That woman will not be satisfied running the nurturing rooms."

"And she'll drive the white coats right off their trolleys."

Beryl marched into the nursery like she owned the place. She passed the egg popping station, where not that long ago she'd hidden and watched; now she was to supervise.

How did it happen? How did she end up working for a mouthy cleaner and five idiots laughingly calling themselves a committee? Who knew as much about test tubes as, well . . . the eggs in the Petri dish?

The room was silent; you could hear a fish gulp.

She breathed in the smell of baby talc, caught sight of the only baby awake eyeballing the solitary fish in the aquarium.

Beryl's stern face loomed into view of the pale-faced baby, blocking out her view of the fish.

The baby blinked.

Beryl stretched to touch. "You're the first," she whispered, "but not the last."

The baby grabbed her finger and clung to the warm flesh. Beryl almost smiled, until she saw the name tag around her wrist.

Casandra Winthrop—that's a mouthful.

She slid the name tag off . . .

"We'll call you Mex," she murmured. "It's short and to the point, just like your nose."

Two women sporting white coats appeared at the door.

They stared at the crumbled name tag.

They had as much time for Beryl as she did them.

She was not a cleaner, but a woman who used to work for "that ex-leader's mob."

"Are you trying to be funny?" said the taller white coat.

"She's the first of a few," said Beryl. "And she needs a name that is something special."

"Pfff—a name like a blender," said the tall one.

"*Mex* is new, crisp, and easy to spell," said Beryl.

"And blends at five different speeds," said the tall one.

The short one smirked.

"Yes, well, when she goes down in the great records of history," said Beryl, "no one will be spelling *her* name wrong."

"It's a baby," said the tall one. "Her future is as blank as a man's appendage."

The short one continued to smirk.

"Very funny. It must be absolutely fabulous to have both brains and wit," said Beryl.

"We do our best," said the tall one. "Why not crack a joke along with a code?"

Beryl let out one of her "*who's in charge*" *sighs*, which went completely over their heads, then looked at Mex.

She had the genes to be great.

---

1. ***Egg Popping:*** an accepted profession. Eggs (also known as valuable real-estate) from a successful woman can earn her a tidy commission.

Chapter Three

PLANET HY MAN'S NATIONAL GEOGRAPHIC

"Manifesto the Great had a heart as big as his appetite and a memory as short as his height. He forgot everything . . . including where he put his underpants."–Beryl

When Bette heard of the name tag destruction, she was livid—who did Beryl think she was?

Beryl was taken to task, which sent her into an intense huffing that could only be done in the dark room where the ex-leader now stayed.

Many women wanted to send him to the Art Centre "along with the other men," but Bette chose to keep him close.

"We need to separate the leader from his subjects," she argued, holding him up in Fanny's old basement along with the "open on command" file cabinets.

It took him a while to stop saying "open"—not an easy thing to do when imprisoned with bugger-all to do.

Beryl stomped into "the dungeon," as the ex-leader liked to call it.

"Don't talk to me of name tags," she snapped.

Silence . . .

She flicked on the light with the impatience of a parent who had spent the last hour looking for her child.

She stared into the half-light of the lamp and sighed. Manifesto the Great's ability to react was on par with a statue.

"I mean who do they think they're talking to?" she said. "Even my hair bow knows more than those pickling *cleaners.*"

"A leader never destroys," he said from a dark corner, "she delegates destruction."

Beryl peered at the silhouette of the ex-leader.

"Have you lost weight?"

"Then," said the ex-leader, "she tells the destroyer what they did wrong."

"You do look smaller," said Beryl.

She stared at the ex-leader's Knee High shadow.

Was he writing?

"If you want to take charge, then forget the name tags and find a comrade," he said.

"You sound like the Librarian," said Beryl, grasping at another lamp.

The ex-leader shouted "open" with a fluster.

She heard a shuffle, fumbled for the switch.

"What are you up to?" she said.

"Nothing?" he said.

"You sound busy," she said.

"Not really just . . . you know . . ."

He rustled.

Beryl flicked on another lamp.

Manifesto the Great, caught like a cat burglar, looked up.

Beryl stared at the book he was clutching suspended over an open drawer.

It was the size of a suitcase—albeit a small one.

He made to slide the book into the drawer like it wasn't there.

He clattered.

The drawer was way too small.

"Here, let me," said Beryl

"I've got it," snapped the ex-leader, trying another drawer.

He pushed the drawer shut.

It sprang open.

Beryl stared at the title: *Planet Hy Man's National Geographic*.

"First edition," he muttered.

"Where did you get it from?" she snapped.

"I have my contacts," he huffed.

"As if," said Beryl.

"Apparently our history is in need of an update."

She looked at him. "But you can't remember what you've had for breakfast."

He glared at her. "I can too."

She flicked a few pages.

"It's all coming back." He grabbed the book.

Beryl eyed him with a *really?* look.

"Yes," he snapped, attempting another futile drawer closing.

He huffed.

Manifesto the Great, now on a meatless diet, was like a recovering alcoholic struggling with his past—wasted years high on meat and cocktails.

It was not a pleasant experience.

His memory had bounced back to bite him like the proverbial terrier, and he had come to the strong conclusion that he was indeed a "tosser."

A tosser who well didn't want to be remembered as one. Who didn't want to think the downfall of men was his fault.

He spent hours editing earlier publications . . . trying to feel better. And when that didn't work, he decided to teach future generations the real truth of men.

Beryl flicked through the pages. "History is written by the victors," she said.

❖

He shrugged, then looked at his reflection in the blacked-out window. *All those years . . . what a tosser.*

❖

Beryl waited until Manifesto the Great fell asleep, then eased the drawer open and stared at the book . . .

❖

Manifesto the Great, or "just call me great," was a man who ruled without favor.

❖

What? thought Beryl. He was a man who didn't listen. W
hen she wrote him a memo, he hurled it at the fireplace. She turned a page.

❖

Fairness was his middle name . . .

❖

More like arsehole, thought Beryl.

❖

Women with power were not to be trusted, but squashed, defrocked, or at least put behind a hoover.

❖

Credit is fluid, Beryl told herself and, with the rub of an eraser, changed "women" to "men"—and, with the flick of a pen, a "Jack" to "Jacklyn."
She smiled.
That's better. Didn't the masses deserve the real thing?
She made a few changes.
She made a few more.
She turned a page . . . laughed, rewrote more, then really went to town . . .
Before she knew it, it was dawn, her hand was sore, and Manifesto the Great was snoring like a walrus.

Chapter Four

THE COFFEE MORNING

"It was voting, but not as we know it."—Voted In (formerly known as a cleaner of public places)

Bette talked of Earth's democracy—a word not many knew of, let alone how to spell.

It was something she had heard of in the institute, and using it made her sound like she knew what she was doing.

"What would a human know?" said a blonde bigwig cleaner. "From what I see, half of them are starving and the other half are singing in movies, calling the world a "grand place."

No one listened.

Bette was talking, and she had a way of "holding a room" with a look you didn't cross, despite a footman's wig perched on her head like a tea cozy.

"They have coffee mornings," said Bette. "And voting."

"Yes, I have heard of that too," said the posh bigwig.

"Didn't Fanny have that sort of tea thing?" said the blond bigwig.

Bette threw her a glare. "We need to include all cleaners."

"Even the outland cleaners?"

"Democracy is not something you do half-arsed, it's an all-or-nothing thing," said Bette.

"Yes, but the scrubbers?"

"There was a time when you were called that," snapped Bette. She strode about the room with a militant march.

"How about a tea party?" said a voice from the back.

"For the scrubbers?" said the blond bigwig.

"Will you stop calling them that?" said Bette.

"Or a caffeine morning," said the posh bigwig. "I could make some biscuits."

"They will run riot. One whiff of that stuff and they'll go crazy."

"Like you lot?" said Bette.

Within a week, a caffeine morning under the "pick a cleaner with a biscuit" campaign was organized.

"Let's meet, discuss, and delegate," she said.

The outback cleaners had no idea what she was on about. The only thing they knew was that Bette's glare was best avoided at all costs.

The meeting was held in the canteen of the Building of Opulence: a building designed to intimidate the ordinary. It was an exclusive place that only a certain class of cleaner cleaned—way above the scrubbers of marketplaces and public toilets.

The cleaners of the outback, unsure of what to do, stopped at the Building of Opulence.

"Come in, Come in" boomed a voice from a speaker.

They trailed through the lobby, stopping at the canteen entrance. They had heard rumors of huge rooms in coordinated colors, plush floors that took all day to polish, and statues so large you could climb to the top and see the outlands, but nothing prepared them for what they saw.

They gasped at the graphic phallic graffiti plastered across the wall and the statue of "hubby" covered in knickers and bras with a thread-bare duster suspended from his appendage—left there as a reminder of the great takeover of men.

"Well, really," muttered one.

"And they're the bigwigs," muttered the market cleaner.

"Shhhh, they'll hear," hissed another.

"Move along," the voice boomed again.

They entered the sleek canteen of the "bigwig" cleaners.

They stared at the shiny tiled floor and silver benches, inhaled the smell of crisp biscuits and luxury caffeine, and looked at each other—some with an "I never realized how shit my life was" glare.

"So this is how the other half clean," muttered the market cleaner.

She looked at her hands.

She had more calluses than the feet of a barefoot trapeze artist. They were as rough as a cat's tongue, so rough she could sandpaper with them. In fact, sometimes she did.

"Bet you these cleaners have hands as smooth as hemp butter," she muttered and was about to say more when Bette appeared by the tea urn, silencing the room.

They stopped, their cups poised at their lips.

They had heard she had the face of a charging solder, the prowl of a hungry lion, and the caustic wit of an Earth comedian, taking no prisoners when it came to heckling, but no one told them she had taken to wearing a footman's outfit.

They stared at her tight silk trousers, ruffled sleeves, and powdered wig and wondered, *What is she thinking?*

"Dunk all you like, comrades," she yelled with a stride.

She made "comrades" sound like an insult and dunking like an illegal act, even though she genuinely wanted the women to dip and dunk.

Bette talked of revolution, equality, and better cleaning equipment.

She eyed her brood, their biscuits untouched.

"Tuck in, there's way more biscuits and pots of caffeine."

"Yeah, but what's the catch?" snapped the market cleaner.

The room was silent. Every eye was on the mouthy market cleaner; keeping her tongue still was like trying to stop a shaken champagne bottle from spraying.

"There is no catch," said Bette.

"*Pfff*," huffed the market cleaner. She turned a pale biscuit in her hand.

"Except, well . . ."

"I knew it." She tossed her biscuit back on the plate. "Let's go, girls."

"Let's not be hasty," said another; the waft of a warm biscuit was getting to her. "I mean at least hear what she has to say."

A few nodded, some with a tentative lift of a biscuit.

They dunked . . .

"Hmmm," said one.

"Arrrgh," said another.

"There's plenty more," said Bette.

"Ohhhh, yes please."

"Don't be bought with biscuits," said the market cleaner.

"Just try one," said her pal with a crisp bite.

"I want representation," said Bette. "A chosen one."

The cleaners, their biscuits poised, stopped.

Chosen? For what?

"One from each sector."

They gulped. No number of gingersnaps could make working with that woman bearable.

"Told you," said the market cleaner.

Bette swiveled to face the market cleaner. "How about you for starters?"

The market cleaner eyed the fine spray of white wig powder on her shoulders. "If it means wearing that, then no thank you."

The women gasped . . .

Bette, taken aback, stuttered, "This? What's wrong with it? Don't you like it?"

"You look like a twat," she said.

Bette's face went blank. She had no idea what a twat was, but she knew enough not to admit it.

"It's the wig," said one.

"Yes, way too . . . you know . . ."

"What?" snapped Bette.

"Well . . . silly."

"Does nothing for you, and as for the trousers . . ."

The cleaners tutted.

"You'd be better with a more flared approach, something that breathed, had a bit of give."

"Yes, well, it's not like we had a lot of choice," said Bette.

"I mean honestly, that silk . . . so yesterday," said a voice from the back.

"We have just taken over the city," snapped Bette.

Silence . . .

"Overpowered the men."

A few shuffled in their chairs.

"Hardly time for a fashion consultation."

Bette threw her famous glare.

"But if you think flared trousers are more important."

The cleaners said nothing.

It was the posh bigwig who broke the silence, poised behind the scenes with a refill of biscuits. She entered.

"Who wants to try my shortcake?" she said in a silky voice.

Not many had heard the smooth accent of the educated. It was as unknown to them as her shortcake and just as delicious.

She slid the biscuits under their nose; they dove in, lulled by the sugary hemp.

"Now," she said, "who's for some delegating?"

Chapter Five

DELEGATION

"Give the workers what they think they want and you walk away laughing; you can always tax later."–Planet Hy Man's National Geographic

With a mouthful of biscuits, the women pushed forward the market cleaner.

Bette beamed (which came across as a sneer).

"Our first Voted In," she said with a comradely pat. "Welcome aboard."

"Who's next?" she said. "Who wants to be part of our new democracy uniting the working women?"

The outback cleaners looked at each other. The biscuits were all gone, the caffeine pot empty . . .

"Pick someone you trust," said the posh bigwig, "who can speak for you."

The cleaners came from five lower-class sectors: the "marketplace," the "office of unimportance," the "implementation of effluent," the "transportation coordinators," and the "preparation of inedible to edible substances."

They split into their groups, quickly ganging up on the most annoying, volunteering them like they were "the best."

Bette was ecstatic.

The posh bigwig, however, had her doubts.

She saw the backward glare of the Voted In as they led the disgruntled cleaners into the footmen's locker room for uniform-fitting.

They looked anything but ecstatic.

And when Bette gestured to the pile of balding wigs, buttonless jackets, ripped trousers, and shoes that didn't match, the Voted Ins seethed the sort of seething that even a blind man could sense.

These five women were the sort to argue, answer back, and scowl, the sort that intimidated, but as they stared at the leftover uniforms, they realized their scowls would be as useful as a candle without a wick.

Everyone was going to laugh at them . . .

"Those two-faced mop-pushers will regret this," said the market cleaner.

"Too pickling right," said another . . .

It was Bette's first mistake.

Chapter Six

PODS

"Equal is what equal does."–Bette

ex and four other babies, who according to Beryl were so special that they should remain at the institute, were separated that summer.

It caused a huge row in the room with a view involving so many caffeine breaks that the other women brought snacks.

"I'm not having any of this high-and-mighty segregation bollocks," said Bette. "We are all equal."

"Equal—that's a laugh," snapped Beryl. "Just because you call the cleaners 'Voted In' doesn't mean they were voted in."

"Actually, they were," said Bette.

Beryl stopped.

She'd forgotten about the "pick a cleaner with a biscuit" campaign.

"Just 'cause you had the luck of leader-minding . . .," said a voice from the back.

"Bit more than minding," muttered Beryl.

" . . . and library-exploring."

"It was more than exploring, I learned bucketloads," said Beryl.

"Yeah, well, you certainly didn't wield any," snapped Bette.

"And learning bucketloads doesn't make you special," said the voice from the back.

"Special? I am so qualified I am overqualified," said Beryl.

"For what? Being a pain in the arse. You're so far up yours you could scratch your tonsils."

Beryl glowered. "You're so equal you're . . . inefficient. Nothing gets down without all this voting malarkey. There is an amendment for everything, can't even flush a john without signing it off . . ."

A few pulled a face.

"All our babies go to the nans—no exceptions" snapped Bette.

"Then we will have a whole generation of soup makers," said Beryl. "How can you train a builder, a mathematician . . .

"What do we need a mathematician for?" said the voice from the back.

"Yeah, what's maths when it's at home?"

"Spending time with a soup maker will make the girls weak," said Beryl, "and the men will take advantage."

"Pfff, hardly; they're getting old," said Bette.

The posh bigwig with a plate of biscuits finally intervened.

"There is more to a nan than soup making," she said.

Beryl rolled her eyes.

"Why don't we do an experiment? See how things work out." She shoved a plate of biscuits between the two women.

She looked at Beryl. "You have your five, and Bette can have the rest."

Bette slid a biscuit between her teeth and nodded as it snapped.

Beryl stared at the plate, and before she had a chance to grab a biscuit, it emptied before her eyes.

"That's fair, don't you think?" The posh bigwig looked at Beryl.

Beryl said nothing; the deal was as fair as the empty plate before her.

That night, she huffed at the leader in his dark room.

Manifesto the Great, staring at his fingernails, said little, waiting for her to finish.

When she didn't, he interrupted with a cough.

She carried on . . .

He spluttered, gestured for some water.

Beryl ignored him.

He poured a drink, sipped, and picked at his nails . . . "She's a bright woman," he muttered.

Beryl stopped.

"Who?"

"Kate."

"Who the pickle is Kate?" said Beryl.

"I think you call her 'that posh bigwig.'"

Beryl eyed the ex-leader.

He took another sip of chilled water; the ice chinked in the glass.

"She knows how to defuse," he said.

"Defuse?"

"Yes, defusing is the right arm of a leader . . ."

He sipped with smugness. "Very important."

"That's the first I've pickling heard of it," said Beryl.

He slid the glass back onto his table right beside an elegant selection of biscuits.

"Along with comrades, which I see you haven't established yet."

Beryl watched as he slid a biscuit between his lips.

It snapped.

"I'm disappointed in you. I hoped you'd be my next LM-2."

"Your next comrade?" said Beryl.

"Well, in a fashion."

Beryl watched the ex-leader polish off another biscuit with an over-the-top "hmmm."

"Looks like you have found your comrade," she said.

"She has potential," said Manifesto the Great.

"That's what you said about me once."

"Yes, well, a leader can get it wrong sometimes."

Beryl said nothing. It wouldn't be long before he would be snoring and she could rewrite, and this time she could really go to town.

❖

Beryl called her five babies prodigies.

The prodigies grew up on the ground floor of the institute within sniffing distance of the kitchen.

They were cared for by two white coats young enough to remember their own childhood in the pods.

White coats, selected by Beryl, who many on Earth would call geeks . . .

White coats who, like Beryl, were fed up with Bette's so-called "we all use the same john" equality.

Two white coats who looked nothing like scientists and more like first-year students still trying to find their way around the university.

Jester, a short woman with a plait long enough for a toddler to touch, had the blank look of someone trying to read a book in the wrong language; Nell, an equally small woman, had spiky hair, magnificent teeth, and a smile to match.

The prodigies in their pods beside the work benches watched the two women . . .

Until they were old enough to sit on a bench, understand a "mind," "leave it" and "hold this" command.

❖

Jester and Nell had the patience of the comatose.

They had spent their early years clutching test tubes and looking under microscopes and, like many women, often wondered about babies, birth, and all that "back in the Dark Ages" stuff the older women talked of.

Teaching a toddler seemed a delicious second best, especially when the prodigies started to question, record, and giggle at the odd joke.

By the time Mex was five, she had heard Nell and Jester's so many times she could repeat them with her eyes closed. In fact, she often did when she couldn't get to sleep.

Jokes about Petri dishes had her snoring in minutes.

Chapter Seven

THE DRAWER

"Bette's cocking up of things made setting women against her as easy as sliding a bow into her beehive."–Mr Ex

*1*948
Bette had pushed her idea of democracy and fairness to the limit, leading to a lazy committee of bigwigs who agreed on nothing, argued over everything, and was so up itself it listened to no one, including the Voted In.

But then who'd listen to them?

Every day, the Voted Ins arrived at the room with a view to find the meeting had been "brought forward," the main business "done and dusted," and any decent caffeine a mere ring at the bottom of a cup.

Their suggestions were squashed and comments ignored, and their so-called uniforms didn't help. In fact, many laughed at them, especially their comrades—the cleaners from the outback. One look at a disgruntled Voted In in her sham of a uniform had them sniggering into their tea trolley.

They stood out as a "poor man's" footman. In fact, that was what they were called, along with "hey you," "you over there," and "that market girl" (despite the fact that only one had worked in the market).

The insults were piled so high the Voted In were ready to take up cleaning again.

They felt as trapped as the ex-leader . . .

Manifesto the Great, now sober with way too much time on his hands, spent his days staring out at his rubbish view with regret.

The last few years of sobriety had not mellowed him but rather made him tetchy, like a grumpy old man with the wrong set of dentures. He had really blown his leadership, and the guilt was not easy to live with. Especially when he learned of men eking out a living in the Art Centre so poor they wore sandals and so defeated they had "let themselves go" with long hair and beards.

There had been the odd male attempt to regain power—men charging into the city screaming "freedom" like something out of *Braveheart*.

The yelling lasted as long as the streets were empty. One glimpse of a woman and men scattered like cockroaches caught in the light.

Weak from years of meat eating, they were hardly a match for the new built-like-a-shot-putter, strong-as-an-ox women.

The women were always prepared; they had lookouts. One glimpse of a male rampage and the whole city was hiding, waiting for the perfect moment.

It was a brilliant pastime, and the women missed it when it stopped—when the men, blaming their inability to "charge like lions" in sandals, gave up.

A few took up protesting, hung placards on the outskirts of the Art Centre, even staged a sit-in—until hunger overcame them.

That was three years ago and the placards, worn, torn, and faded, still flapped in the wind over the head of the one remaining protester. No one had the heart to remove the placards, let alone the protester.

He had been there so long his hair was down to his waist, his loin-cloth as loose as underpants with buggered elastic.

He was nicknamed the Guru, despite saying little apart from "piss-weak tea," which was usually followed by the tossing of said tea.

Manifesto the Great never thought he would see the day that the only hope for man's freedom lay in the hands of a man as snarled as a century old tree with barely a handkerchief covering his bits.

There was a time when that Guru was a big strong oaf of a footman.

Manifesto the Great was almost too bitter to care, until Kate came into his life.

A woman with a hopeful quality and a way of talking with questions —asking his opinion, which Manifesto the Great found irresistibly endearing.

He could sit with her for hours and spent most of his time trying to manipulate just that.

It was Kate's job to "go between," as Bette called it.

"It's a tough job but someone has to do it," she said. "And that pickling Beryl has as much ability to 'go between' as a mechanical rat has to procreate."

A few women laughed until they realized Bette was not trying to be funny.

Three years of ruling can do that to a woman, and any trace of humor had long gone with Bette.

She even stopped visiting Jack and John in the institute; their idea of advice was to give the planet "ten years *max*" unless something was done about the planet's energy crisis.

The *something* being a sort of "harnessing"—advice as useful to a ruler as a used teabag.

Manifesto the Great watched as Kate entered his room with a small bag of biscuits seductively swinging from her hand.

He spied hemp chocolate and sighed.

Kate's handmade-one-at-a time chocolate biscuits were something else.

"Jack and John say we have years rather than decades," she said, tossing the bag his way.

"What do you think?"

He nodded, sliding his hand into the bag. No one asked him much, and like one of Kate's biscuits, he intended to savor it.

"I take it you're talking of the energy issue?" he finally muttered with a spray of crumbs.

She nodded.

"So, breeding babies takes more energy than first thought?" he said.

"It would seem so," said Kate.

"I did say," he said.

"Did you? I thought it was that so-called Guru," said Kate.

He looked at her.

"It's not the energy you need to worry about."

"Oh?" said Kate.

"It's your well-fed, lazy committee."

"Bit rich coming from you."

"The masses are fed up."

"How would you know?" said Kate.

Manifesto the Great talked of the "energy cuts," the "rationing of fires," and the "controlling of cooking." "Hot food is but a mere memory," he said, "apart from that piss-weak tea."

"But those were your cuts," said Kate.

"And what's worse, what really boils a worker's blood, is you lot tucking into freshly baked biscuits with caffeine from Earth—freshly ground by the thighs of virgins . . ."

"Don't start that *virgin* bollocks again," snapped Kate.

". . . caffeine so delicious you're silenced for hours," said the ex-leader, finishing with a venomous bite of his biscuit.

Kate watched a few crumbs settle on his chest.

"Don't see you complaining."

Manifesto the Great reversed his chair, moving nearer to Kate.

"Those in the institute are starting to panic," said Kate. "And Bette has no idea, except to, well, clean and yell."

"You could always get the men back," he said.

"Men?" said Kate. "But they're past it, as useful as barbecue in the rain."

Manifesto the Great stopped as the memory of a barbecue lingered; he almost drooled.

He eased his wheelchair closer, cornering Kate against a filing cabinet.

"I think the answer lies in the sun," he said.

"That's not what Jack and John say," said Kate (another of her go-between assignments).

"Hmmm . . ." he said.

"They talk of harnessing," said Kate.

"Like with a woman?" Manifesto the Great smirked.

"Talk like that and you'll end up in the Art Centre—or worse," said Kate.

"There's a worse?" said the ex-leader. He grinned. "Am I *opening* up a whole new can of worms?"

A drawer flew open, pushing her toward the ex-leader.

She swore under her breath.

"Perhaps the answer lies on Earth," said Kate.

She pushed the drawer shut.

Manifesto the Great turned to the mirror. Earth was in the middle of the Olympic Games; a cycling race was on.

"Them?" He laughed. "What could they possibly know?"

"I have heard they are quite inventive," said Kate.

"They still use push power. Not like us, with these fabulous drawers that open with a mere word."

A drawer flew open, catching Kate's hip; she toppled into the ex-leader's lap.

Kate, with a hard shove, stood up and snapped the drawer shut. "If you say that word one more time, I am leaving and never coming back."

"You'll always come back."

"If I do"—she glared at him—"I'll take these cabinets with me. There must be better things to do with such drawers than trying to corner women."

Chapter Eight

JACK AND JOHN

"Democracy, it seems, is all right for some."–The one formerly known as the market cleaner

*J*ack and John were in the bowels of the institute, reading meters.

Things had come to a head.

The institute was in a pickle over the energy crisis, and frantic women were not something Jack and John were trained to deal with.

"We need to find a way of harnessing things," said John.

"Harness?" said Jack. "Like in a woman?"

John looked at him. "Talk like that and you'll end up in the Art Centre or worse."

"There's a worse?" said Jack. "You see that place? The men are as defeated as a squashed banana."

John didn't answer. He had heard that joke so many times he could spell it backward.

He returned to the meter, wrote down a few figures, began to calculate, and stopped.

Beryl had burst in the laboratory next door with her usual dramatic entrance.

Jack rolled his eyes.

Beryl was always charging in, catching "*her*" girls off guard, usually with a "taking over the planet" idea. She had been demoted to a "Voted

In apprentice" for refusing to dress as the others and now saw her chance—all she had to do was find a new source of energy.

Buzzing with new hope, she made her way to the logbooks and pulled one down with impatience.

No one looked up.

She page-flicked with high speed, swore, tossed the book aside, and pulled down another so ancient the pages were almost brown.

"Is there nothing of energy in these pickling books?" she snapped.

Jester and Nell, peering into microscopes, didn't move.

The prodigies, precision-smearing on glass slides, carried on.

While Mex, bent over a blocked sink, pulled out a plunger.

Beryl glared at her girls, who were poised on boxes to reach. "Am I invisible?"

Nell nudged Jester. "See this? In a few days' time, opening this will clear the room."

"Wonderful," chuckled Jester.

"I could empty a building for days with it. Just one wave—one particle."

"Marvelous."

Beryl stopped. "Particles, like in energy?"

"Mold," said Jester. "It's the beginning of things . . ."

"Cheese for starters," said Nell.

"Cheese but not as we know it." Jester winked at the prodigies.

The prodigies giggled.

"I don't have time for cheese," snapped Beryl.

"Toastable—like in the good old days," said Jester.

"Promises," chuckled Nell; the prodigies laughed.

"Why are you laughing?" snapped Beryl. "We have a crisis."

"Ah yes, the great cheese drought," said Nell.

Mex began to plunge the sink.

Suck, suck, suck . . .

Suck, suck, suck . . .

"And if we don't get this new dairy-free cheese up and running, there'll be hell to pay."

Mex threw her weight into plunging . . .

Suck, suck, suck . . .

Suck, suck, suck . . .

"The way things are going, there'll be nothing to toast," said Beryl.

"Nothing?" A prodigy stopped. "Nothing?"

"There's an energy crisis," said Beryl.

"Pfff, that," muttered Nell. "It is but a mere pickle."

Suck, suck, suck . . .

"Will you leave the drain?" snapped Beryl.

Mex, with a glum look, stopped.

Beryl feigned a smile.

Mex scowled.

"I am talking of our future," said Beryl.

Suck . . .

Beryl threw a glare at Mex.

Mex, with an insolent look, dropped the plunger to the floor.

Nell peered into her microscope. "Future? What is a future without cheese?"

"Forget about the cheese," yelled Beryl. "We are running out of time, and the city wants to know what the pickle the institute is doing about the crisis."

"Hardly; they're all watching their mirrors," said Nell. "The Olympics."

"Pfff—men on push powers."

The women pulled a face.

"You know, bikes pointlessly speeding around a track like a life depended on it. What could that possibly have to do with our energy crisis?"

"A man in shorts is a sight to behold," said Nell.

"Hold? Me thinks you jest," said Jester.

"Jest, me? In a white coat—how could that be possible?"

"You'll be jesting on the other side of your face if you don't get a wriggle on," snapped Beryl. "One day, my picture will be on the 'wall of leaders.' You should keep in with me."

"A picture is just a picture, easily removed," said one of the prodigies.

"I'll be running things and making all the right decisions."

"Right decisions are only right upon reflection," said another.

Beryl threw her a look.

"I'll be basking in my glorious leadership—looking at the view from the top." She paused. "Just need to sort the energy first . . ."

"And what's wrong with the view here?" said Nell. She stopped.

The women looked outside at the slag heap by the bike shed. The shed door was propped open with an out-of-date rusty bike that hadn't seen a bum for years, let alone a bit of oil.

A mechanical rat, poised on the stump of a seat mid paw-cleaning, looked up, blinked, and scurried away.

For the first time, the two white coats could not think of a joke.

"That bike is going nowhere," muttered Mex.

"Nowhere?" said a prodigy. "But the pedals still work."

Chapter Nine

WINSTON CHURCHILL

"Affluent meat-eating saps a man quicker than bloodletting."– Manifesto the Great

It was a comment that would change everything, a comment that would set Beryl on a course that she would call her destiny. It was like a light went on . . .

As the prodigy talked of a turning wheel creating energy, Beryl's mind sparked into action. *Harnessing.*

"Whip me up a bike," she said.

"Does it not need a circuit track?" said Jester.

"I not talking of racing—I'm talking of stationary, connections and, well, harnessing."

Mex, mid kicking, stopped.

"Harnessing . . . is that not what they did with women—years ago?"

"Harnessing can apply to many things," Beryl said with a weak smile. "And I was thinking of energy"—she patted the prodigy's head—"thanks to you."

"A gym?" said a prodigy.

"Men peddling?" said another.

"In shorts?" said Jester.

"Short's optional." Nell laughed.

Even Beryl smiled.

The white coats looked at Beryl. "It could work."

Beryl nodded.

"And convincing the men?" said Mex.

The women looked at Mex like she was talking Swahili.

"Who said anything about convincing?" said Beryl.

Jack and John heard it all.

"Told you to clear up that mess, sort the shed," snapped John.

Jack looked at his comrade. "I guess there are worse things than the Art Centre now."

A few hours later, Beryl, staring into her mirror, was taking notes as old footage of Winston Churchill, suited and booted, flooded her screen.

She stopped, pressed pause, and thought.

He could really make a speech work . . .

Her lip tilted into an almost-smile.

If such an ugly man in a gangster suit could move the masses, then what could she do in such a suit?

She turned to her shoebox-sized closet. Picturing herself on the speech balcony dressed in black, she pulled out every pink belt, shoe, and jacket and hurled them out her window.

"Vengeance is mine," she shouted into the dark alleyway.

A mechanical rat dodged a shoe.

An old lady, spying another, made a sporty lunge.

Others stopped, dodged, then rummaged.

While Beryl emerged with her hair dyed black and a mean look on her face. She peered out at the women riffling through her things.

Bette's days were numbered, she told herself. She was as buggered as the half-chewed cigar perched between Winston Churchill's lips.

❖

Kate poured Manifesto the Great a caffeine.

"Beryl used to tell me caffeine beans came from the thighs of a virgin." He laughed, waiting for a reaction, perhaps another "bollocks." He loved it when Kate said "bollocks."

"No woman likes to visualize a virgin, especially grinding her thighs," said Kate.

"Manifesto the Great laughed. "How little you know, pumpkin."

"It's Kate," said Kate, brushing his hand from her thigh.

He was just about to try again—higher—and she was just about to give him a slap when the door flung open and Jack and John appeared.

"Beryl's plotting a coup," said John.

"They're planning to use men . . ." said Jack.

John threw him an "I'll do the talking" look.

" . . . in the worst possible way."

The ex-leader stopped. "What? Make them clean?"

"Way worse," said John. "They are talking of—"

"Bikes," jumped in Jack. "Stationary bikes. And she's quoting Winston Churchill."

"Shit," said the ex-leader.

"Bollocks," said Kate.

"This Winston Churchill sent men to their death—on planes. Is that what she is planning?"

"No, it's bikes and energy."

"My men, energy slaves?"

"They are hardly your men," said Jack.

"Shut it." John nudged him.

"Get me my footman," said the ex-leader with a longing look at Kate as she headed out the door.

❖

Bette looked out onto the courtyard below. It was busy, full of bustling women heading to work. She stopped, catching a glimpse of two bigwigs whispering in a corner.

Those women are as bribable as a man, she thought. *And they think I have no idea, that I'm stupid—I've seen them yawning while I talk, laughing at my recycling ways.*

She turned to Kate. "So, she's talking of bikes."

"Well yes, and using men."

"Hmm . . . how quaint."

Kate looked at her. Since when did a cleaner say "quaint"?

"I can see the merit in her ideas," said Bette.

"But men? They are hardly robust; they get about in slippers from what I've heard."

"Sandals," snapped Bette. "And it didn't stop them fighting back."

"A few placards with *'freedom'* scrawled across is hardly fighting," said Kate.

"They had their sit-ins," said Bette.

"One old git hurling tea at crows is hardly a sit-in," said Kate.

"It's a start," muttered Bette.

Bette had turned a blind eye to the rampaging of men and was glad when it stopped, but she couldn't turn a blind eye to Beryl's idea. Despite it lacking any democratic ideals, it was an impressive one and, she hated to admit, the only one.

She sighed. Besides, democracy's not all it's cracked up to be; in fact, it has ruined many women.

She eyed Kate. Apart from her.

"Maybe we can turn things to our advantage."

"With men?" said Kate.

"We could give them some hope," said Bette.

Kate tutted.

"I don't think it is hope that Manifesto the Great is looking for."

Bette pulled a face.

"Is he still cornering you with those drawers of his?"

"Yes," said Kate. "I told him any more of his squeezing nonsense and I am out of there, and I'm taking those cabinets with me."

Bette stopped; she'd seen them in action, and she knew of Kate's technical inability. She had a way of turning a wholesome idea into something destructive.

"Maybe we can use those cabinets to our advantage," said Bette. "You talked of making them into a beverage centre."

Kate face lit up. "Well yes. He laughed, of course—like he always does."

"Well, let's make that Beryl laugh on the other side of her face as well," said Bette. "And make a killing into the bargain."

Two days later, under the instigation of Bette and one too many squeezes from the ex-leader, Kate called in the removal robots.

Manifesto the Great sulked; then, after the last of the file cabinets were finally wheeled out the door, his sulking turned to vengeance.

"Never trust a machine to do a woman's work," he yelled to the back of a removal robot, and when no one answered, he yelled again, this time vowing to get even.

Chapter Ten

THE PASSAGEWAY

"Who knew that a man's thighs would be the planet's only hope—until, that is, something better came along."–Kate

Beryl flicked off the mirror mid movie.

"Design me something black with a tie," she said, "like in that gangster film."

The Voted Ins looked at her. "Jimmy Cagney?"

"What about Winston Churchill?" said the market cleaner.

Beryl nodded. "I'm talking black and large, something that makes us look muscular."

"But we are muscular," said Voted In One.

"A look that screams 'a force to be reckoned with,'" said Beryl. She looked at her crew. "If we want our bikes to be taken seriously."

They nodded.

"To save the planet."

"Well yes.

"Then we need to look intimidating, imposing, and yet intelligent."

The Voted In, sourcing material from old curtains, did their best and were soon strutting about the room imitating James Cagney and E. G. Robinson.

They couldn't wait to wear their new look, parade in front of their peers, "wipe the smirks from the outback cleaners and silence the jeering bigwigs."

Beryl, however, had other plans . . .

"Hang them up," she said. "In fact, hide them."

The Voted In stopped. "What?"

"You heard: hide them."

The Voted In looked about, confused and disappointed.

Voted In One began to whimper.

"Timing," said Beryl. "A coup is all about timing."

"Who said anything about a coup?" she blubbered.

"We need to prepare the public first—get them on our side. It's all about conditioning," said Beryl. "Paving the way."

"We are not building roads, we just want to walk about without being laughed at," said Voted In Two.

Beryl talked of a future when a suit would stand for control, power, and a footman's uniform would mean nothing but—a servant.

"If you do what I say," she said, "we will have the masses on our side and Bette ousted without a drop of blood."

"Who mentioned anything about blood? I just want to be called anything but 'hey you,'" said Voted In One with a sniff.

Beryl laughed. "Those bigwigs won't be calling you anything soon—they'll be waiting on you."

The operations room was on the ground floor with the Trolley Hygiene room at one end and the worker's beverage centre at the other.

It was a plain room with not much going for it except for a window the size of a fist and a wall of books, *Wife-ie's Emporium* being the largest and oldest. A tatty-looking catalog that no one noticed until, one day, they needed a doorstop and realized the catalog wasn't a book at all but a lever for a secret door.

Apparently, a male, unknown, had a passion for gothic stories and spying.

The door led to a hive of passageways from the good old days when Wife-ie advised and the Librarian didn't need a wheelchair. Fanny used it, Mr Ex used it, and now the Operators used it.

When Bette took over, three cleaners were installed to watch and learn from the male Operators—and get rid of them "as soon as feasible."

The women, however, had other ideas. Sharing a screen can do that to a woman.

The passage was the perfect place for "getting rid" of men and yet keeping them, and with it being secret, there was no need to "clean up."

In fact, the tunnel was a bit of a mess.

Years of "she's coming" hissed through the door, sparking a tossing of a paper cup or a hemp stump, had left its mark.

As instructed by Beryl, the Voted Ins walked into the Operations room to find two Operators poised over the monitoring.

The Operators didn't look up. They were, just as Beryl predicted, in the middle of sorting films for the masses: musicals and, well, more musicals.

"Just put the tea over there," said one with a wave of her hand.

The market cleaner, poised for a smart-arsed, answer stopped. *Was that moaning from behind the bookcase?*

"Yes, yes, yes!" yelled a voice.

The Voted In looked at each other. *Yes?*

The two Operators, oblivious to any noise, continued with their writing and tuning.

"Just close the door on the way out," muttered one.

The Voted Ins, accustomed to taking orders, left and shut the door. Then they stopped with a "wait a minute, what are we doing?"

They barged in, stopping in their tracks to see a third Operator looking disheveled, yet glowing with another Operator pulling a hemp stub from her hair.

"Just leave the tray by the bookcase," she muttered without looking up.

"Do you see a tray?" said the market cleaner.

The Operator turned swiftly, taking in the tatty footman's uniforms.

"No, but I see an outfit that screams 'tray bearing.'"

"We come from the room with the view."

She eyed the hole in the market cleaner's jacket. "Yeah, that'll be right."

"With orders for a change in films."

"Pfff, as if—they love their musicals," said Operator One.

"It's the costumes," said Operator Two.

"Exactly. They are fed up with the costumes," said Voted In Two.

"Look," snapped Operator Three, spitting a hair from her lips. "If you're telling me that the likes of *you* can tell the likes of *me* what to put on that screen, then you can think again . . ."

She stopped.

Soaring like a skyscraper from behind the heads of the Voted In appeared Beryl's beehive. It was so high she had to dip at the entrance.

The Operators stared at the dinner plate of a bow fastened at the front.

Anyone brave enough to get about in that hairdo had to be, well . . . fearless.

It wobbled as Beryl pushed forward, leaned across the desk, and tuned the screen to a gangster film.

"Let's have more in suits," she said. "Keep the masses happy."

"What?"

"Let's give 'em suits, guns, and some violence."

Within weeks, the masses, fed on a diet of gangster films, began to admire the suit. There was something uncomplicated about it. Men strode, ran, jumped in cars, and pulled guns from their suits—way more impressive than tight silk.

In fact, the price of silk dropped like a knicker with no elastic. No one wanted it anymore. What they wanted was something that made them feel like a man.

Women started to improvise, making ties out of napkins and hand-kerchiefs, secretly painting mustaches on their faces and pulling pretend guns from their pockets—just for a laugh.

It wasn't long before a footman's uniform was old hat, black trousers were in, and 'James Cagney' was on every woman's lips.

Bette, her head full of plans to sort Beryl once and for all, had no idea—until she headed into the room with a view to find her girls merrily cheering on Humphrey Bogart.

As he pulled out a gun, she stopped.

A removal robot crashed into her back with an "excuse me" bleep.

"What the galaxy is going on?" she snapped.

Humphrey Bogart pulled the trigger, the gangster collapsed, Bette winced.

"This is what you watch when I'm not about?"

"It's all the rage, ma'am."

"Here's me thinking up a surprise for all your hard work and you're lounging about watching men . . ."

A larger removal robot appeared, pushing a filing cabinet straight into the back of the first robot, jolting Bette off balance.

"Are we moving?" said Bigwig One.

Bette, regaining her footing, shook her head.

"This is going to be the making of us."

The bigwigs watched the robots deposit the cabinets against the wall.

"Kate's idea," said Bette, rubbing her back.

The bigwig looked at each other. Kate's ideas were as useful as a box of matches in the rain.

"Caffeine machines," said Bette.

"Machines for beverage?" said Bigwig One. "What next?"

"Men have guns," muttered a voice from the back.

"No more kettle-flicking—just a shout and there you are," said Bette.

"I was quite happy pouring my own," muttered Bigwig One.

"Me too," said another.

"Open," shouted Bette.

The bigwigs jumped as the file cabinets closed in on them like Dr Who Daleks.

They panicked, attempting to escape the room.

"Way better than a few pistols," said Bette with a maniac look at the voice from the back cowering in the corner.

Chapter Eleven

LEGLESS

"A shoe hurled at the speed of light makes an excellent missile."– A dodging mechanical rat

When Manifesto the Great's footman was called, he was gobsmacked. The last thing he wanted to do was help, let alone set eyes on his so-called leader again.

He was quite happy in the Art Centre, blissfully inspired. No more uniform, and—thank the gods of the galaxies—no more standing to attention; he could lounge around to his heart's content watching the young men saunter in sandals, and when not discouraging the useless attempts at a coup, he was making things.

He had a thing for taut bottoms, long legs, and various other appendages and had taken to sculpturing his newfound pal, the long-legged footman. Who, like him, thought there were better things to do than uselessly run into the city yelling "freedom" with a wild look and a mop of unruly hair.

"It's the sandals," said the long-legged footman, clutching a broom.

"Hold that pose," said Manifesto the Great's footman—or Mr Ex, as he now liked to be called.

"I'm no longer a footman," he said, sparking a great name change for many, including "Well Hung," who had the short of chin that swung below his jaw like a pair of pajamas; "Lumpy," who had lumps where no one should look, and of course "the Guru," who looked so old that every birthday was considered his last. He shuffled rather than saun-tered and coughed with almost every breath. In fact, many ran when they saw him coming on account of his ability to cough on par with a sprinkler.

"Sandals are for sauntering, not charging," said the long-legged footman.

"I said keep still," muttered Mr Ex.

"Leave the strutting for women, that's what I say," said the long-legged footman.

His arm wavered.

Mr Ex tutted . . .

"And hold that stick like it's a sword. This is to be an inspiring piece, not a portrait of a cleaner."

"Oh," said the long-legged footman; he braced himself. "Like this?"

Mr Ex, admiring the view, smiled.

He looked at his work. Carving out of soya mash had its problems, mainly the drying: it was just so damnably quick. But it was almost finished. *Just a little nip here* . . .

"There's talk of an upstart," said the long-legged footman.

"Hmmm . . . just in the middle of the crucial bit," he grunted.

"And *your* leader . . . wants *you* to intervene."

"Oh, puff and piffle," snapped Mr Ex as his nip crumbled into a hack.

"That's what he said as well," said the long-legged footman. He wobbled.

"Pfff—a crisis to him is no wood for a barbecue," said Mr Ex, furi-ously polishing his hack.

"Apparently he is off the meat and talking sense," said the long-legged footman with a wobble.

Mr Ex sighed.

"Take a break," he said with a useless toss of his knife. It bounced off the sink.

The long-legged footman flopped into a chair.

"We can start again tomorrow," said Mr Ex retrieving the knife with a grunt.

"Tomorrow? Aren't you going to . . . ?"

"What?" snapped Mr Ex, thrusting his knife under a tap.

"You know . . ."

"Save the world?" muttered Mr Ex.

He looked at his muse. "In a tracksuit?"

"Well yes."

The long-legged footman rubbed his arm. He dreamed of saving men from sandals and floppy hair, returning them to their former glory, back to the days when they made decisions.

"I mean who wants to spend the rest of their life like this . . . ?"

Mr Ex grunted. Scrubbing soya mash off a knife was not easy.

"I am quite happy, thank you," he said.

"Happy? You want us all to end up like the Guru?"

"Pfff, him—that's what way too much fasting on hemp tobacco does to you."

"I want to resurrect him," sighed the long-legged footman, "to the magnificent . . . whatever he was."

"He *is* still alive," snapped Mr Ex.

He glanced at his model. "And there are plenty of other things you could erect."

The long-legged footman, ignoring Mr Ex's smile, moved to the statue and stared at the front.

"I'm sure he didn't always live in loincloths."

He stopped . . .

He eyed the groin.

"Did you create this from imagination?"

Mr Ex, with a hot blush, coughed. "You do have a lot of socks down there."

Chapter Twelve

THE SPEECH

"It was the 'gangster' that swung it, that inspired the new women in a black suit."–The Voted In formerly known as the market cleaner

Beryl eyed her reflection. The last few weeks had gone just as she'd planned.

The stage was set, her time had come, and she was going to make the most of it, get in early, overwhelm the room with a view before they were sidetracked by Kate's posh biscuits.

She slid on the crisp jacket and posed. It set off her shoulders to a tee—screamed control.

She liked the black suit; striding in it was a breeze and way better than the footmen's outfit.

Beryl turned, looked around at the bustling basement. Under a sea of bubble wrap were bike frames, templates, and flat-pack packaging. In the middle were Jester and Nell, entertaining the prodigies with jokes and popping bubble wrap while irritating the Voted In and Mex. And on the opposite wall, ignored by all, the Olympic cycling was playing on another large mirror.

The market cleaner frowned at Beryl with a "pfff." She looked as happy as a mechanical rat under the heel of a shoe.

The black suit was her idea.

Was it not her who came up with a suit even better than James Cagney's getup?

"What about us?" she said.

No one heard; they were too busy trying to read Nell and Jester's instructions.

"Does that not just go in there?" said Voted In Two.

"If you want to cycle with your tongue," said Jester with a *pop* of bubble wrap.

The prodigies giggled.

Mex glowered.

Voted In Two gestured to the Olympic cycling. "Aren't we making those bikes?"

"That, my love, is a wheel in forward motion," said Jester with an exaggerated *pop.* "We are creating a stationary."

The market cleaner grabbed the bubble wrap with a "give me that."

Beryl didn't hear. In her head was her speech, a speech that was going to turn all against Bette.

She turned back to her mirror, *which was her best side . . .*

"We shall cycle on the beaches, on the landing grounds, in the fields and in the streets; we shall cycle in the hills . . ."

"What?" said the market cleaner with a glare at Beryl's back.

"We shall never surrender," said Beryl.

"Surrender?" said Voted In Three with a look of panic.

"Until a new Planet Hy Man with new power steps forth to rescue and heat the old," said Beryl in her Winston Churchill voice.

She turned to face her comrades with a "what do you think?" look.

"I'd cut the voice," said Voted In Two.

"Definitely," said Voted In One.

"Pardon?" said Beryl.

"Bit old hat," muttered Jester.

"We shall cycle at dawn . . ." purred Beryl.

The women looked at each other. Even Jester and Nell lowered their tools.

"Bit corny."

"At dusk in the landing fields . . ." she yelled.

"Landing fields?" said Voted In Two.

Beryl stopped. "It's a figure of speech."

The women looked at her.

"From Winston Churchill," muttered Mex with a dark look.

Voted In Three choked on her water. "Winston Churchill?" She looked to her comrades. "Is the crisis really that bad?"

"Apparently," muttered the market cleaner.

The lights dipped.

Beryl looked at her comrades. "If we don't saddle up these men soon, then the lights will be out before you know it."

The Voted Ins looked at her with a "you mean us?"

"The time for suits has come, girls; we are going in, and we are not coming out until the takeover has, well, taken over."

When Beryl entered the room with a view, the bigwigs feigned surprise.

They stared at her dark suit, the thin knot of her tie. They had heard of Beryl's gangster look, but seeing it in the flesh took them off guard. It was, well, impressive.

Beryl looked about for Bette.

The door crashed open.

A tea trolley clattered in, followed by Beryl's *suited and booted* crew.

They squeezed into the room.

"Where's the funeral?" muttered a voice from the back.

"This is no funeral," said the market cleaner.

"Not now," said Beryl.

"This is our future in the making."

"I said not now—we need to wait for Bette," said Beryl.

"Energy on tap," said the market cleaner with a dramatic pull of the cloth.

The bigwig cleaners stared at the mini stationary bike, their jokes stifled by the ingenuity of it; it was a stunning idea.

"This is our future: high tech, innovative, and so much more."

"Shall I minute that, ma'am?" said a despondent male voice with a sigh.

The women turned to the doorway.

Standing to half-hearted attention, clutching a walking stick, stood a wigless man in a tracksuit and sandals and sporting a five-o'clock shadow.

It took several minutes for all to recognize the ex-leader's footman.

"Minute?" said Bette, appearing from behind. "We've something better than that."

Beryl's stomach lurched. *Bette knows?*

Chapter Thirteen

FILING CABINETS

"One man's codpiece is another man's jockstrap."–The Guru

The Voted Ins moved forward, spoiling for a fight.

Beryl threw them a "hold your ground" look, then turned to her rival.

"What would you wager for an energy solution?"

"Wager?" snapped Bette. "What are you? Earth's Robin Hood?"

"Robin Hood?" shouted another male voice. "Look no further."

The women turned to see the long-legged footman appear from behind Mr Ex.

A young man with a thin nose and legs so long he looked like an ostrich, he had something—a Robin Hood something—despite the sandals.

Beryl stopped in her tracks.

He caught her eye.

She held his stare.

"Who are you?" said the market cleaner, a woman with no time for Robin Hood–type men.

"I speak for the men," he said.

"Who cares?" said a voice from the back.

"All of 'em," said the long-legged footman. "Every single one." He pulled a pose and grinned. "The whole kit and caboodle."

Mr Ex sighed.

He knew it was a stupid idea to involve the long-legged footman, but Manifesto the Great had insisted.

Mr Ex had argued, claiming he was too old to save the plight of man, but would the ex-leader listen?

"It's your job to save men. The last thing they need to be doing is riding bikes on that swill those women call food."

"But sir . . . I've just started my latest statue. I don't have time for all this hero malarkey."

"Statue?" The ex-leader stopped. "What an excellent idea: take him with you, that footman with the long legs. His strutting will shut those women up."

Mr Ex had his doubts. The long-legged footman had illusions of grandeur, a big mouth, and an ability to spread his affections way too wide. Him sticking to any script, let alone one person, was as likely as getting that stupid ex-leader to listen.

He looked at the long-legged footman eyeballing Beryl. Their job was merely to remove the suited women, not make some ludicrous speech about Robin Hood.

"Stick to our arrangement," he hissed.

"Perhaps we can put those legs of yours to good use," said Beryl, pushing the trolley just shy of his heels.

A wheel squeaked.

"I'd rather be legless," said the long-legged footman, "than let my men take orders from you."

"I wasn't talking of the men," said Beryl. "I was talking of you, Mr . . . Legless."

The women gasped.

Manifesto the Great's footman dropped his walking stick.

Beryl in a suit was quite impressive, and *Legless*—what a name.

"Open," shouted Bette jumping from the file cabinets.

The cabinets sprang into action . . . crashing the trolley into a wall.

Beryl watched her miniature bike tumble to the floor; its spokes crumbled under a filing cabinet.

She and her comrades didn't stand a chance.

❖

A few hours later, Bette and the bigwigs, still in the room with a view, watched Kate oiling the filing cabinets and checking for repairs.

In front of the bigwigs, Beryl and her Voted Ins were rounded up like sheep . . .

Except there was no sheepdog, just filing cabinets circling about the women like Dr Who Daleks, their drawers opening and shutting, poking them with robotic jabs.

The pain of a drawer's jab was bad enough, but the humiliation was way worse.

Defeated, shamefaced, and ridiculed, Beryl and her Voted Ins were tied up and paraded through the street with two footmen behind them, one strutting like a peacock and the other, looking as old as Wife-ie's obelisk, hobbling with a walking stick.

They retreated to a small room by the laboratory; the crushing of their bikes would not be forgotten in a hurry.

"Well done, Kate," said Bette.

Kate looked at her comrade with a "ma'am?"

"The cabinets," said Bette. "Excellent job. I had no idea you could be so devious."

Kate blushed. She didn't have the heart to tell the truth: that the reconstruction was a miscalculation. She had been aiming for a beverage maker, not a destroyer; it was Bette who saw the potential.

When she first saw the file cabinets jolt into action, Bette jumped for joy.

As the others dove out the door like stunt men, Bette clapped her hands with glee as the shuffling cabinets trapped Bigwig Two . . .

"Excellent," said Bette.

"Help!" shouted Bigwig Two.

Kate grabbed a stick and, as she pulled Bigwig Two out, wondered for the first time about her leader.

Had things gone to her head?

"Yes, well, we all have our talents," muttered Kate.

"Beryl is minced soya thanks to you," said Bette.

"That wasn't exactly my plan . . .

"You have ruined a revolution, nipped a revolt in the proverbial. You deserve a new mug."

"Here," snapped Bigwig One, pushing a mug forward.

Kate squirmed. "I don't think that's necessary."

"Well, Herself over there does," sniffed Bigwig Two.

The others eyed Bette's "real hero" mug. Sipping with that cup took caffeine to a whole new level. They knew; they had tried it and were seriously pissed off.

Kate deserved a pat on the back like they deserved a hole in the head. She had stumbled on the idea like she always did . . . and while Bette thought charging filing cabinets was the bees' knees, they thought otherwise.

Bigwig One gestured to the crumbled miniature gym in the corner flattened like a napkin.

"Beryl did come up with a good idea."

"Don't mention that name."

She picked up the flattened bike and slid it on the table with reverence. "Could save our energy crisis."

"I think you'll find that was . . ."

Bette stopped with a blush.

"The fellow . . . with the long legs?" said Bigwig Two.

"Legless?" Kate huffed, returning to her oiling. "I wouldn't believe him. He's as fork-tongued as, well, a fork."

"He'll come in handy," muttered a voice from the back.

Bette eyed the remains of the papier-mâché bike. Thanks to Kate, she was prepared, able to think ahead and bribe.

Not that it took much.

Legless was all for it.

❖

Legless took Mr Ex's mission and grabbed it with both hands, he knew how to make the most of things and had exactly the right broom closet to do it in.

Bette hadn't been in a broom closet since her cleaning days, but Legless's cryptic message had her intrigued.

"Just give me one bike and I'll have that street of yours lit up like a barbecue."

"I'm going in," she told Kate and, despite Kate's misgivings, found herself pressed against a broom with Legless's warm breath at her neck.

"Just one bike?" said Bette.

"Not one," said Legless. "A fleet."

"A fleet of bikes?"

"Gyms."

Legless moved closer. "Power unimaginable."

"I can imagine," she stuttered.

"Earth-watching for all."

She said nothing.

"Rations a past memory . . ." he whispered close to her neck.

Bette caught her breath .

"Oh?"

" . . . and heating a given."

Bette, making a mental note never to meet Legless alone again, eyed Bigwig Two brushing the tattered pieces of the gym into a shovel.

Getting out of that broom closet wasn't easy. In fact, if it weren't for Kate's knock on the door with a "Beryl is here," she might have lost herself completely.

A warm breath on a neck can do that to a woman. Especially a woman like Bette, who hadn't been touched since, well . . . she couldn't remember.

She threw a weak smile at Kate, then noticed a jacket left behind.

She slid it on and drew herself up straight. Neck-whispering would be impossible in this.

She turned to her girls. "We could make more of these, couldn't we?"

Kate stood up, rubbing her hands clean.

"The jackets?"

Bette nodded.

"All we need are a few curtains and a template," said Kate.

The bigwigs rolled their eyes.

Bette smiled.

"So much for Winston Churchill," she muttered, looking at herself in the mirror.

"What?" said Kate.

"Never mind," said Bette.

Turned out making energy from a gym was a breeze, as easy as knocking up a few gangster suits from a pair of old curtains.

The men weren't exactly ecstatic.

"Shove it up your Lycra," one yelled. "I'm not sitting all day on a bike getting a pile of piles while they heat up their homes."

"Yeah!" yelled another.

Legless promised beverages on par with the room with a view.

They grumbled.

"We were promised better food."

Silence . . .

"Athlete's food."

"Pfff—as if," jeered a few.

Legless took them to the first gym.

The men looked unimpressed.

He jumped on a bike. "Look, it's easy," he said, "like milking a four-legged creature."

The men pulled a face; a few stomachs turned.

"Must you be so earthy?" said Mr Ex.

Legless bounced on the seats. "It's so soft your butt will be massaged—all day."

"We're to sit on that all day?"

"There will be rotas," said Legless.

"Who cares about rotas and arse-massaging when your joints are creaking?"

Legless stopped and gestured to the seat between his legs. "Here is where all the power is."

The men pulled a face.

"Not there, but here." Legless gestured to the bike. "While we're firing up their straighteners, we can plot."

The men looked confused.

"Then, *boom* . . . a strike."

The men started to catch on . . .

"When they least expect it."

The men started to nod.

"And a whole new world."

"Hear, hear," they said.

"With us at the helm."

"Hear, hear!" they shouted.

"Ours for the taking," yelled Legless as the men cheered.

Manifesto the Great heard all about it, and with a grim face and a hand firmly on Kate's thigh, he muttered to himself.

"Bette says we'll soon have an army of babies," said Kate, shoving his hand away.

Manifesto the Great said nothing. Cycling was the sort of thing that could age a man.

Chapter Fourteen

BROOM CLOSETS

"Hell has no fury like a woman misguided with a sausage."–Mr Ex

Legless took his new name, along with the new gym, in stride and ran with it.

He was smart, and he knew he could find a way out for himself and the lads. After all, *they* were only *women*, and he was close to their leader.

Despite Bette's refusal for anymore "broom closet meetings," she happily took his advice, sometimes even allowing him into meetings.

Kate had her reservations, but she was outnumbered by the bigwigs and their "Let's have more of him" demands.

Under Legless's neck-whispering suggestions, Bette insisted on a democratic rustling of men into gyms, along with cycling food, chilled water, caffeine, and the sort of Lycra worth a second look.

The food designed by the institute gave men energy, muscles upon muscles, and clear skin, the Lycra a sense of pride, while the caffeine screamed 'status.'

It wasn't long before men were queuing up to ride for their country.

Legless took one look at the firming of a man's butt and saw an opportunity: a glass gym. "Let the women see us in our glory," he said.

Mr Ex had his reservations, but Legless was too full of himself to listen.

"A tight butt is temporary," said Mr Ex.

"Pfff," said Legless. "Bette and me are like this"—he crossed his fingers—"and I have those bigwigs eating out of my hand. Soon we'll be in their homes, and before you know it . . ."

"Yes, I know—*boom!*" Mr Ex sighed. "No one takes a good body seriously."

"These women do—they are starved of a six-pack. They are queuing up to watch us."

"But what happens when the wrinkles set in?"

"Hormones," laughed Legless. "The food of youth. I'm younger by the day."

Mr Ex looked at the tight skin across the face of his muse. Cracking a smile on that face was as likely as cracking a nut open with your tongue; who knew what it did to their insides.

"I wouldn't feed a four-legged creature that stuff," he said.

Legless laughed. "This butt and this face is my . . . our way out."

Women stopped to watch the riding men and were soon making contact eye.

Apparently, looking at a man's six-pack was good for women's health, as was a butt you could bounce a penny off; many women were willing to pay for it, buy their own personal energy provider.

A stationary cyclist in one's own home became as "in" for the upwardly mobile as a mirror in each Earth room.

In fact, watching one's cyclist heat one's straighteners was the height of, well, opulence.

The young men worked their arses off.

With a decent body, they could be riding in a sunlit lounge, chilled bubble water at their elbow, caffeine breaks, hot showers, Lycra that breathed, and if they were lucky, a bit on the side.

All they had to do was be seen by a successful upwardly mobile woman and hook up—as simple as shoveling effluent.

Working in the gym gave men the sort of body Lycra was made for.

Leg parades sprung up all over the city, which young men happily joined. They posed, pouted, sucked in their breath, and when that didn't work, they slid rolled-up socks down the front of their Lycra.

An old trick based on the "titillation is half imagination" theory.

A theory the likes of Mr Ex laughed at.

"If a woman is expecting steak for breakfast, you can't offer her a sausage and expect to get away with it."

The women never had it so good . . .

For the men, however, it was different, as staying young was not as simple as taking a few hormones.

Hormones weren't all they were cracked up to be, and they couldn't stop the effects of all-day cycling forever.

It took a few years, but when effects of cycling took hold, the women were ruthless.

The first sign of a wrinkle, a hint of breathlessness, a Knee High delay in the heating equipment, and the personal rider was tossed aside like yesterday's soya. There were plenty more men to pick from.

The golden age of cycling came and went quicker than the crumbling of a biscuit.

The rejects staggered back to the Art Centre warning of cycling abuse.

"They only want our energy," said one bandy-legged fellow.

It didn't take long for the wrinkled ones to band together.

They picketed the leg parades, stuck leaflets on the glass walls of the gym demanding the right to cycle in private, and when that didn't work, they tossed their socks in piles and burnt them.

Legless bided his time and tried to reassure. "Not all women are so fickle," he said. And when that didn't work, he promised a plan: "All I need is another broom closet and a willing bigwig . . ."

Chapter Fifteen

SOCKS

"Making a man a slave is as easy as picking a nail."–Bette

Six months of sock-burning had Bette staring out the window wondering what had gone wrong.

She listened to Legless, and when that didn't work, she marched, paraded, and bellowed in suits with shoulder pads as wide as a barn door, and did that stop 'em? Make a difference? They still burnt their frigging socks.

It was time for something different, a new phase of ruling, a better plan.

Kate joined Bette at the window.

In the distance, they could see smoldering smoke at the feet of Wife-ie's obelisk.

"Socks, I presume," muttered Bette.

"Legless calls it a mere skirmish," said Bigwig One.

Kate rolled her eyes.

"I've seen bigger skirmishes on a toilet seat," said Bigwig Two.

"Ignore it. They're bound to run out of socks," said Bigwig Two.

"A skirmish is never something to ignore," said Bette.

They watched the men dancing around a couple of red coals.

Kate looked at Bette's closed face. "We could shoogle them out of the city like the others."

Bette threw her a glare that would stun a gangster.

"Shoogling is too good for them, besides they'd just come back." She sighed. "Like fungus. We need to make a stand, let them know who's in charge."

"Legless says—"

Bette turned on Bigwig One. "And where is he?"

She stopped catching sight of Legless attempting to douse the flames.

The other men jeered.

"Pointless—that man is absolutely pointless," muttered Bette.

She turned to her girls.

"Herd them."

"What?" said Kate.

"You heard: herd them."

"The men?" said Bigwig One. "Like animals on earth?"

"Yes, enslave 'em."

The women gasped. *Enslave?*

Bette flashed a manic look. "If making a man slave is what it takes, then by the gods of galaxies, that's what we'll do."

"But they are one of us . . . aren't they?"

"If we don't control them, they'll take over, start all that neck-whispering malarkey."

The women had no idea what she was talking about.

Bette blushed. "I mean, we'll run out of power, end up breaking our necks in the dark."

No one said anything.

Bette sighed. "There'll be no more Earth-watching."

"Pfff, that . . ."

"Your implements will be as dead as an appendage," she snapped.

Silence . . .

"Or worse, you'll be heating them up yourselves."

They looked at her.

"On your own bike," she yelled.

❖

It didn't take long for the women to agree—about as long as it took Legless to fire up a pair of straighteners.

❖

The herding took the men by surprise. They were completely unprepared.

They scattered, cowering in all manner of places: under market stalls, in wardrobes, under transporter bonnets and up trees, listening in the dark to the rounding up of slower men.

The slower men were hauled by the scruff of the neck, paraded down the street, shunted into gyms, strapped to stationary bikes, and ordered to ride.

"Run away. Head for the hills," the faster men whispered, scurrying to the outlands like smoked-out mechanical rats.

The fieldworkers were having none of it; they wanted these useless men like they wanted beehive hairdos. They had no time for men young, old, or middle aged, and inspired by the great Celts terrifying the Romans, they chased the men, screaming like banshees.

"Off with their heads, their underpants, and all that's beneath!" they shrieked.

The fieldworkers were scarier than a dark night in a minefield, scarier than standing on stage stark naked with a stomach full of laxatives, and way scarier than any stare Bette could muster even when shrieked awake from sleep.

Rumors flew of fieldworkers ripping ears from mechanical rats to use as broaches, playing hopscotch with the balls of men, making slings with their dangly bits, and stealing into the city to shout into the sleeping face of Bette, scaring her so much that she had to change her knickers.

It appeared that being a fieldworker required the sort of facial expression that would terrify a polar bear.

❖

In the end, the free men, with no other place to hide, cowered in the Art Centre.

THE LABORATORY

"Getting what you want is not always the answer."–The Apparatus of a Woman: Volume One by Legless

Ten years on

The years of Beryl walking into the laboratory and being greeted with a welcome were a distant memory. Gone were the days when the prodigies scrabbled to please her, hung on her every word. She could shout herself hoarse, pick at their work all day; it didn't make any difference.

The prodigies were teenagers, and her entrances were greeted with silence.

Apart, that is, for Mex. She scowled.

Beryl tried to befriend them, telling the girls they were *special* and had a place *in the scheme of things—and did it work?*

They didn't even look at her.

Beryl's entrance had as much effect as the ex-leader had on the city, and every time she was ignored, a little piece of her died . . .

Mex, unlike the other prodigies, was not a geek; she was a kicker, dreaming of action, not inventing. She saw her first "herding man parade" when she was eight and couldn't get enough of them. Her biggest nightmare was for the men to run out by the time she was old enough to herd.

And while the others ignored the funny ways of "her with the expanding beehive," Mex could not hide her feelings.

The older she grew, the less she laughed, and by the time she was fifteen, she hardly smiled, not even Jester and Nell's jokes. One jokey quip about the smell of moldy specimens had her scowling on par with Bette.

What was funny at three and irritating at ten was annoying at fifteen, and jokes like Beryl's annoyed Mex like a poked rattle snake.

For years Beryl had barged into the institute shouting, "You're a prodigy, not a kicker," and Mex was as fed up as an impotent sperm donor.

She wanted to kick the stupid bow of that stupid beehive into the air like a polished turd.

Beryl stared out the window. Mex had been sent outside to "cool off." It was not the first time she had been pulled up for test tube tossing, and something had to be done.

The women watched Mex attack the recycling pile with a kick so high and so swift she *just* missed a mechanical crow.

"That Mex has as much insight as a pizza," muttered Jester.

Beryl sighed; she had such high hopes for Mex.

"There must be something we can do," said Jester.

"With that scowl?" said Nell.

Several more crows appeared, defending their comrade.

Mex sent them flying.

The ground was carpeted in feathers. Puffed and sweaty, Mex spat out a feather and swore.

"It's not the scowling we need to worry about," said Beryl.

"Indeed not," muttered Nell and Jester in unison.

A few hours later, Mex, standing in Beryl's so-called office, was listening to yet another "explain yourself" lecture.

The office—a lean-to on the side of the shed—was a compact affair with an envelope-sized window, a fold-up table and chair, and floor space so small that Mex could smell what Beryl had for her elevenses.

The only remotely big thing in it was the aquarium, hijacked from a market stall under the "tax or take something to the equivalent" law.

In fact, it was under the same law that Beryl "helped herself" to the lean-to and the chairs and table. It was Beryl's attempt to establish some sort of rapport with her prodigies, not that it worked.

What they were working on was way above her head, and reviewing their work was merely a farce. Apart from Mex.

Mex, silent and sullen, couldn't even be arsed to explain why science was such a big yawn for her.

Beryl never listened.

"You *are* science," said Beryl. "You have been programmed to get excited about equations, not to fail every exam like a dyslexic half-wit male."

She slid Mex's last exam across the desk. "Try to remember you are a prodigy, not a kicker."

Mex pulled a face. "I prefer to kick."

Beryl sighed. Then, as she always did at such moments, she stared out the window.

"What was it this time?"

"They were laughing at me."

"All scientists laugh."

"I *said at* me."

Beryl turned to her, scrambling for an answer.

"Yes, well, kicking *was* the downfall of many a man."

"But fresh air and punching helps." She glowered. "You should try it."

"Enough," said Beryl, attempting a stomp. "You have privileges, and you should make the most of them. Knowledge is power."

"So is a whip," said Mex under her breath.

"What was that?"

"Nothing," said Mex, wondering how long this *farce* was going to take.

"Why can't you be like the others," said Beryl, "and study?"

'Cause I'm not made that way, thought Mex.

Beryl waited for an answer with her best glare.

"You're going to have to do this again," she said, gesturing to the exam.

Mex huffed.

"And you'll keep doing it till you pass."

Mex rolled her eyes.

"And I don't mean just pass. I mean with gold stars."

"Pfff, who cares about stars?" muttered Mex.

"What?" Beryl stopped.

Jester's head appeared through the curtain.

"Ma'am, we have an incident . . ."

"Can I go now?" whined Mex.

"No, I'm not finished," snapped Beryl.

"But—"

"Just wait here."

Mex, eyeing Beryl's disappearing back like it was a pile of crow droppings, pulled a face.

The curtains closed.

"Bette wants an audience," said Jester like the curtain was soundproof. "With you."

Mex eyed the overfed fish loitering about the bottom of the aquarium. She tapped the glass; the fish stopped, then moved toward her finger. She sprinkled food onto the water.

"Am I supposed to jump?" said Beryl.

"Best to take things calmly," said Nell.

"Calm? I'll give her calm—right up her backside. Who the pickled egg does she think she is?"

"She said something of a rebellion," said Jester.

Mex watched the fish rise to the surface. She dipped her finger into the water. A fish touched it with its mouth like a kiss; she chuckled.

"Rebellion? Who? What for? I don't understand."

Nell looked at Jester. "I think it was the men."

"Men!" snapped Beryl. "They are fed and watered. What more would *they* want?"

Chapter Seventeen

REBELLION

"Honestly, give a man a view and it goes to his head."—Verruca

*L*egless, cheering the men on, cycled like a demon, his fit legs perfect for the job.

Ten years on, Legless had grown from a man with ostrich legs to one with the sort of legs that required a second look, a gasp, and a yearning to touch. And as for his butt, it was, to quote an earthling, "poetry in motion, sex in Lycra."

Not that any in the gym appreciated it.

The men bitched, especially when he started shoving thick industrial socks down the front for extra "titillation," although who he was trying to titillate was anyone's guess.

Legless still believed in the pull of a butt.

The others, however, had seen where that got them and laughed. Still, he could motivate, and his push-ups were to die for . . . as the lead cyclist, he was a given.

He had an annoying positive energy that no one could compete with, and he had a scheme.

He had learned from the past; this time it would be different.

He had a plan, and Beryl was pivotal to that plan. She was desperate to overthrow, and he still had a butt that could manipulate, a tongue that could persuade, and he was the king of neck-whispering.

❖

Mr Ex, on the rowing machine behind, pulled a half-hearted row. He was fed up; not even the taut backside of his model could cheer him up.

Not that he had much chance of *that sort of thing* these days.

Recycled hemp and soya were necessary cogs in the new energy program, and there was bugger-all left to sculpt. It was as easy to get hold of as Legless's attention. He had turned into a real arse-licker.

In fact, if Mr Ex didn't know better, he swore he caught Legless flirting with an outback cleaner *who did anything but clean.*

If he was younger and had more energy—well, if he had any—then he would actually say something, but all he could do after a day's rowing was gulp insipid tea before flopping into bed.

Mr Ex paused, wiping his forehead, as the Guru shuffled to the water cooler.

"Come on, lads," yelled Legless, moving to a standing position. Sweat rolled down the small of his back.

Mr Ex sighed. There was a time when the sight of that backside had him whistling in his tea, where the trickle of sweat had him wondering *how far?* . . .

Not now. He couldn't even raise a spit let alone a whistle, and as for wondering, the only thing he pondered was how long it would take for his legs to stop aching.

The gym exhausted him as much as it seemed to energize Legless.

No one thought of what would happen when the men were too old to move.

"Did you hear?" Well Hung, now stick thin like many of the men, coughed. "Did you hear?"

Mr Ex, with a "here," tossed him a tissue.

"There are rumors of the ex-leader getting hitched."

"Hitched to what?" snapped Lumpy.

One laughed. "A wheelchair?"

"A heart defibrillator?" puffed another. "He's so knackered his joints crack jokes."

"Come on, guys—less talking, more cycling . . ." yelled Legless.

"The only thing he can raise is an eyebrow," said Well Hung with a weak punch at the water cooler. "A fumble for him is as possible as this thing filling a cup."

Mr Ex stumbled from his rowing machine and, with a kick that had him red-faced, spurred a trickle from the water cooler.

Well Hung, catching the dribble with a paper cup, eyed it like it was liquid gold.

He sipped with an "arrrgh . . ."

"Aye, Kate's 'going between' has truly turned him lovesick, like an Earth movie."

He stopped.

Manifesto the Great appeared, clutching an overnight bag, the headless obelisk of the Librarian, and an extra-large, first-edition, pseudo leather-bound copy of *Planet Hy Man's National Geographic, Volume One*.

His wheelchair squeaked to a halt.

Manifesto the Great's hand had finally strayed too far, and Kate had had enough.

"There is going between and going between," she said. "And between my legs is far from one of them."

Manifesto the Great had minutes to think, pack, and grab, and not in that order (hence the obelisk).

"Hitched?" said the ex-leader. "The only thing I'm hitched to is these two bozos here."

Jack and John appeared.

They, making the mistake of suggesting that "a man can only discover the boundaries of a woman by pushing them," were told to take the Librarian's chair, *along with* the ex-leader, and not return.

Ten years of constant questioning under the glare of a woman can do that to a man, especially when that woman was once an equal—of sorts.

They had outlived their teaching, educated themselves out of a job and decent caffeine, and, like all great male scientists, they were eventually stripped of their white coats and led away.

❖

Jack, with a grunt, pushed the ex-leader into the gym. The tires were as flat as a day-old buck's fizz.

The ex-leader turned to Jack.

"You could help."

Jack shoved the wheelchair, sending the obelisk toppling to the ground.

John picked up the obelisk and dumped it on top of the cooler.

The cooler gulped, gurgled, and, after a series of bubbles, sent a surge of water from the tap.

Well Hung thrust another paper cup under the downpour, then handed it to the Guru curled up in the corner.

"Piss weak," muttered the Guru snatching the cup.

"What are we going to do with him?" Lumpy gestured to the ex-leader. "He's dead meat."

"A poor turn of phrase," said Legless.

"But it's true." Manifesto the Great sighed. "I've bunions the size of pumpkins—I can hardly walk let alone row."

He stared into the gym. What had he done to deserve this?

Granted he had no idea of her middle name, how old she was, or whether she was married. In fact, he had no idea what she did to make his life so smooth until she, well, left. But this? A gym packed with sweaty men—did he really deserve this?

The Guru skulled his water, then upended his empty cup on his head.

"If he's dead meat, what's the Guru?" hissed a voice from the back.

The Guru coughed, spat, then pulled an "up yours" gesture at the voice from the back.

Legless peered into Manifesto the Great's book.

It was so large it needed a table to open on.

He flicked a few pages and, with his usual annoying positivity, said, "He could always read while we pedal."

Over the next couple of days, the ex-leader read aloud the exaggerated history of Planet Hy Man to the men, entertaining them with witty comments, jaunty expressions, and hilarious impressions.

He read of Wife-ie's implausible antics, James the Strong's love of harlots, and the Librarian's wig collection.

"Who makes this stuff up?" he often said, his eyes wet with laughter.

"A woman's imagination," muttered Well Hung, "hormonal as the making of milk."

Manifesto the Great was having the time of his life. It was as good as making speeches. Even better: the writing was so far-fetched, so laughable . . . until that is, he arrived at the "Beryl" chapter . . . his so-called assistant/mentee.

The wife of Manifesto the Great was held by all as the revolutionary who freed women.

The ex-leader stopped and looked around the room. "What wife?"

"Think they've mixed you up with your father," said Legless.

"Pfff, him?"

"Maybe skip a few pages," said Mr Ex with a puff.

The ex-leader carried on . . .

It was she who noticed the changes soya inspired in her friends. "There could be something in this whole soya issue," she said to her husband.

He ignored her for the last time.

She was fed up with his "I'm too busy to listen" and angry at his "I need a shag now" gropes, which were always followed by an "

I'd be better off doing it myself" comment . . .

"Me? Grope? Do it myself? As if," huffed Manifesto the Great.

He tossed the book on the floor. "Outrageous!

I am going to revolt."

A few of the men chuckled.

"Go on strike."

A few more laughed.

"At least rewrite."

"Take it easy," yelled Well Hung, "can't be that bad."

The ex-Leader glared at him. "A leader never gropes . . ."

"Aye, but you ain't one now, are you?" said Lumpy.

He picked up the book, began to read, then stopped . . .

"Well, go on," snapped Manifesto the Great.

Lumpy, with a gulp of discomfort, read on . . .

. . . she worked incognito, until she found a way to self-fertilize an ovary. Semen was out the window and Petri dishes were in.

❖

The men stopped. Some gasped . . .

❖

Just a couple of strokes, that's all it took . . . and man's future was doomed. Although they didn't see it at the time. Men thought a woman free from months of pregnancy would have time for other things . . .

❖

Well Hung, poised by the water cooler, forgot the tap. Water trickled onto his foot; he jumped, closing the tap without thinking.

"Knew they'd take the credit," Jack muttered to John.

❖

Some men thought a free woman would be happy to wait for them to come home—even talk dirty on the phone.

❖

"Dirty talking—on a phone? First I've heard of it," snapped Lumpy.

❖

Some men saw the writing on the walls; without meat hormones, many became indecisive and weak.

❖

The Guru started to chuckle.

❖

Many just gave in . . .
The Guru let out a laugh.

❖

. . . and women took over.

❖

"It was a bit more complicated than that," said Manifesto the Great.

The Guru roared with laughter. He was a man who liked writings and philosophy, which is what comes from wearing a loincloth.

No one took him seriously, so Guru tried to make every word count.

"That's fighting talk," said the ex-leader.

The men stopped. *Not again* . . .

"Are you talking negotiations or petitions?" said Well Hung.

"Bugger negotiations, stuff the petitions—I'm talking rebellion, revolt, and serious yelling. I trusted her. So much for loyalty."

"You did dump her for Kate," said a voice from the back.

The ex-leader huffed. He was angry, which is what comes when you lose everything to a woman you didn't notice who you thought was your loyal servant.

"No one rewrites history and gets away with it, especially when it comes to me."

Mr Ex looked at Well Hung. "Does he know these walls have ears?"

Chapter Eighteen

EGG CARTONS

"Bette's stare was way worse than her shout."–Kate

For ten years, Bette was terrorized by the fieldworkers' "night frights."

When they would happen was anyone's guess. Bette could have weeks, months, years of peaceful sleep, then *bam—a* scream, a yell in the middle of the night, followed by those god-awful tongue-poking painted faces, kookaburra hair, and a scream that would startle the comatose.

It was not the first time she had to change her knickers, and when word got out . . . her credibility was in tatters.

How the story broke, no one had any idea, but Bette had to do something and called Beryl for a secret meeting at dawn before the *other idiots* had even thought of their first caffeine.

Beryl took her time.

Ten years of being ignored can do that to a woman—a woman who had tried to help.

Bette had no idea how to run things, just as Kate had no idea how to sort out the wandering hand of an ex-leader. And when Beryl suggested, warned, or muttered an "I told you so," she was treated like an old git with the memory of a pea.

Sauntering was too good for her.

She strolled into the leader's john.

"So where's the rebellion then?"

Bette, scrubbing her underwear with vigor, didn't look up.

"We'll build a wall," she hissed.

"For a revolt?"

"Like the Great Wall of China. That'll keep the so-and-sos out."

"But we have a wall," said Beryl, milking the moment.

Bette scrubbed. "That so-called *hedge* wouldn't stop a wheelchair with a flat tire, let alone those marauding Celts."

"Fieldworkers, ma'am," said Beryl.

Bette stopped, tossed her scrubbing brush at the sink, and turned to her rival.

"Fieldworkers smield-workers—who cares? Just build a wall. I'm fed up with them and their invading. I mean what do they want? They are fed and watered."

"But what about the rebellion?"

"Did I say rebellion?"

"Well, yes."

She wrung out her underpants, hung them on a rail, and looked at Beryl.

"I'll make it worth your while."

Beryl eyed the dripping underpants.

The leader was mad, off her trolley. A fruitcake would make more sense than her . . .

❖

John was skeptical of Legless's strike.

Aging men in tracksuits staging a revolt were as believable as Legless's sock down his trousers.

Jack, however, had other ideas.

He had a brain bolt of a plan. "Thinking on his feet," as John liked to call it, Jack had squirreled away a variety of implements in his trousers when escaping, and now he knew what to do with such implements.

"We need to communicate with the other gyms," he said.

He gestured to the walls. "Without anyone hearing."

The Operators not only heard, they also saw it all. When the cleaners took over the room where the Operators------*operated*, they took over the spying of not only Earth but Planet Hy Man as well. The gyms had more surveillance cameras than a shopping mall.

They watched Jack lead John into the gents' and chuckled. As if that wasn't bugged; it was the first thing they did when the gyms were set up.

Jack stood by a urinal and pulled John closer.

"Shhhh."

"I haven't said anything," hissed John.

Jack stuck his hand down his own trousers.

John pulled a face.

A urinal flushed as the door crashed open.

Manifesto the Great filled the doorway.

"Put that away." His voice echoed across the tiled walls.

He stopped, his wheelchair wedged in the doorway.

Jack produced an egg carton.

John pulled a "what the pickle" look.

"We could make connections," said Jack.

"With an egg box?" snapped Manifesto the Great, attempting a reverse maneuver.

"Shhhh, everything is bugged," hissed Jack. "You can't even fart without an audience."

"But do they know that we know?" said Legless.

The men stopped.

Legless appeared from a cubicle with his annoying "what's up, lads?" smile.

"And what if they do?" said John.

"Who cares? It's an egg box!" yelled Manifesto the Great.

Legless looked at the egg box. "I thought those things were combustible."

"They are," said Jack. "It's what's inside them that counts."

He emptied the egg box, laying his precious communication implements on the bench.

"It's something Kate was working on."

Manifesto the Great stopped. "Kate?"

"Yes, she had this idea for portable communications."

Manifesto the Great lifted the wristbands.

"Easy enough to produce and even easier to hide," said Jack.

"That woman's inventions are never what they seem," muttered Manifesto the Great.

Legless lifted the soya glue hardened over the tip of a tube and turned it in his hand.

"Nothing a bit of hot water won't cure," he said.

"I wasn't speaking of the glue," said the ex-leader.

The Operators, no longer chuckling, looked at each other and agreed to draw straws as to who would tell Bette.

By the time they had found some straws, Mr Ex had the mother connection up and running in the headless obelisk. And by the time Bette was stewing over her deluxe, triple-roasted caffeine, Legless and his lads had a small production line in the gents', and the Guru, dressed as a woman, was strutting from gym to gym connecting the men with devices so small they could be hidden in mugs and so loud that a mere belch could be heard miles away.

He thought it was the funniest thing since Beryl's creation chapter.

A few days later, Beryl, sporting her new *black* look, appeared at Mex's bunk bed.

"I think," she said, "your talents are better suited to boots and training."

The other girls looked up, rubbed their eyes, and gasped. *Beryl, first thing in the morning, in the bunk room?*

"Ma'am?" muttered one.

Beryl held up a hand to silence her.

"I knew you were something special," said Beryl. "But I never thought it would be kicking and the like."

"Kicking?" muttered another of the girls.

"Yes." Beryl turned to her prodigies. "Some use microscopes to change the world; others, like Mex here, use brawn."

"Anyone can do sit-ups."

"Yes, but how many can, with the precision of one kick, remove a Petri dish lid from its dish without one crack?"

"That's stupid."

"Not anymore," said Beryl.

She looked at Mex.

"Pack your things and come with me. There is a wall out there with your name on it."

The next morning, standing in Beryl's lean-to by the shed, Mex was listening to the rant of a woman desperate to take over and a crazy plan about a wall . . .

"The leader has gone mad," said Beryl. "She wants a wall."

"So I heard."

"By the hedge."

Mex looked up. "And the fieldworkers?"

"That's where you come in."

"I do?"

"Yes, you need to spy."

Mex huffed . . . she wanted to herd, not spy.

"Spying's for whimps, tossers and pickling men" she said.

"Not when you're going to build an army."

Mex stopped.

"To guard the hedge."

Mex almost liked the idea . . .

"And I was thinking of those quarry turtles. All you have to do is put them in the right place under the hedges."

Mex stopped. It was not that long ago the quarry turtles were stopping Beryl.

Chapter Nineteen

THE QUARRY

"Opening up the closet of a woman's imagination is the downfall of many a man."–The Apparatus of a Woman: Volume One by Legless

*B*eryl stood at the cliff top of the scrapyard and stared down at *her girls*—although they did not see themselves as hers.

In fact, when they saw her, they turned their backs. The Voted Ins blamed her for everything.

Their 'suit' ideas had been stolen, their patterns and diagrams seized, the gym they constructed taken over and reproduced all over the city, while they, shamed as traitors, had been sent to the scrapyard to work. Their 'Voted In' title now a dirty word, an insult thrown about like a used duster.

Ten years on, they were still angry, and the only thing that made it bearable was the idea of getting the better of Beryl and the whole damn committee.

"Incoming! Incoming!" squeaked a high-pitched mechanical voice.

Voted In Three pulled a robot torso from the pile.

"What about this?"

The other two stopped.

"A Mae West?" said Voted In One.

Voted In Three nodded, brushing a wisp of hair from her eyes.

"Well done."

"Beryl alert! Beryl alert!"

Voted In One looked up.

"What does *she* want?"

"Who knows? Who cares?"

Voted In Two gestured to the wheelbarrow. "Quickly."

The Voted Ins had spent the last ten years recycling the robotics left over from man's reign. Dismembered Mae West and turtle robots were taken to Jack and John's old shed, which had been moved to the quarry and deconstructed for reuse (one of Bette's better recycling plans).

It was a job they hated, until they discovered the Mae West's all-thinking, all-speaking microchip embedded in her torso.

With the Mae West robot era forgotten as quickly as a bad cold, they jumped at an idea.

The torso was their ticket out, a gift from the galaxies . . .

Reconstructed to handbag size, with her chip upgraded, a Mae West torso became Planet Hy Man's first (albeit cumbersome) H-Pad (which many claimed was the prototype for Earth's iPad), and it could earn a tidy sum.

The women, saying nothing, quickly brushed the torso down and slid it onto the wheelbarrow.

"Beryl alert! Beryl alert!"

"Hurry," said Voted In Two, "we need to get this to the shed before she comes."

"You'll be lucky," said Voted In One, gesturing to Beryl.

Beryl was still on the edge of the cliff, a miniature turtle robot circling her heels at the speed of light. Losing that thing was as easy as handcuffing a fly.

The robot was, at first, one of their ingenious ideas. One of the first collaborations with Jester and Nell, a collaboration born from a distrust for Beryl.

Known as "the biter," the turtle, inspired by an Earth Rottweiler, was designed to bite and not let go—like a mousetrap.

At first it was, literally, a howling success; watching Beryl clatter down the cliff like tumbleweed had them chuckling in their tea for months.

Until Beryl mastered the art of tumbling . . .

Arriving one day to catch the market cleaner mimicking her with an askew tea urn on her head and a breathless "that turtle will be the death of me," Beryl vowed to "make 'em eat their words."

She trained like an Olympic gymnast for weeks, rolling and cartwheeling like a hyperactive ninja. Soon her entrances were more mountain goat than tumbleweed.

With her black beehive sprayed to cement hardness that could deflect a cricket ball, Beryl swerved, ducked, and dove, clocking every rock and mudslide.

Beryl soon perfected an arrival with hair as erect as a wicket stump and not a skid mark in sight.

Catching sight of her girls heading off with a wheelbarrow, she pulled away from the robot and charged down the slope.

The Voted Ins carried on like they hadn't seen her.

The turtle followed. Beryl turned and tutted, then rolled a rock his way.

He ducked.

She tried another.

The Voted Ins walked faster.

The turtle, his memory chip now in overdrive, swerved like an ice skater.

She cartwheeled over a mudslide.

He jumped.

She somersaulted over a fallen trunk.

The Voted In picked up speed, breaking into a trot.

The turtle pulled a skid and, with his famed three-point turn, cut her off.

The Voted In whispered a cheer.

Beryl pulled an emergency stop.

The turtle reared on his hind legs.

She, with a swift kick, knocked the turtle onto its back, its legs air-running uselessly.

The Voted Ins, deflated, turned to each other.

No matter what it did, a turtle could not roll from its back.

"Always the back roll," muttered Voted In Two.

"Told you," muttered Voted In One. "Stopping that woman is but a mere pipe dream."

❖

The shed, unlike its lean-to, was large and comfortable and had a caffeine machine.

In fact, it was so comfortable that Jester and Nell often retreated there. Mex and the prodigies were at that "you're an idiot" teenage stage, and they had as much disdain for Jester and Nell as the Voted In had for Beryl.

Jester and Nell were bent over a turtle hump with the intensity of a bomb squad when the Voted In barged in like said bomb was about to explode.

Jester and Nell didn't look up.

Voted In Three grabbed the hump with a "quick, hide it."

Nell grabbed it back. "We're just at the final stage."

"Only a few more tweaks," said Jester.

"Tweaks? We've no time for tweaks! Beryl will be here . . ."

Jester and Nell stopped.

". . . any minute," snapped Voted In One.

"Shit."

Drawers opened, torsos disappeared, turtle shells upturned, and egg boxes reappeared. Diverting Beryl was their only hope.

The door creaked open.

They jumped to their places . . .

Beryl glared at the Voted Ins, bent over benches like they had been at it all day .

"That goes there," said Jester to Voted In Three, feigning concentration.

"I thought we agreed that the egg boxes were way too combustible," said Beryl.

Silence . . .

Beryl stopped. She picked up an egg box. It was glued to another wet, oozing *something*, which flopped to the ground.

"What is the point of this?"

Nell stopped, faking surprise with an "oh, it's Yourself."

Beryl huffed, looked around for something to dry her fingers with. "Where's the market cleaner?"

"Picking up egg boxes—the city goes through them like toilet paper."

Beryl pulled a face, gesturing to the pile of uselessly glued egg boxes. "Hadn't we agreed to mash them into something useful?"

The women looked at Beryl with their best innocent look.

"The committee wants more intercoms," lied Voted In Three.

Beryl eyed her girls. She could smell four-legged shit a mile away . . .

The intercom box, recycled from no-longer-needed egg cartons, was the brain wave of the blonde cleaner.

Having worked in the institute from an early age, she saw the rise of "eggs with everything" until birds became mechanical.

For years she walked past the egg box piles outside the kitchen, and one day, inspired by a Bette's "sustainable" rants, she thought, *This will shut her up*.

Beryl turned the crumbled egg box in her hand and thought of the good old days, when the word *scramble* set a mouth watering.

The only thing scrambled now, thought Beryl, *are these women's stupid stories*.

She looked at her girls.

"The intercom project has died on its arse and you know it."

Silence . . .

"And they blame you."

Chapter Twenty

ASSETS

"Ten years ruling a bunch of women who had an opinion on everything would put even a socialist off democracy."—Bette

"Blame us? For what?" said Voted In Three.

"Apparently, they are combustible," said Beryl.

"We did tell them that."

"One blew up in the kitchen, leading to the mass destruction of Kate's biscuits," said Beryl.

"Pfff—when have *we* seen a biscuit?"

"They said you owe them," said Beryl. "And now they want you to make a Great Wall."

The women stopped, thinking of the hedge-like affair on the outskirts of the city brown under the burning sun.

It was so hot that the fieldworkers used the hedge for drying clothes. It was as much a border as the remains of the Roman wall in Britain. In fact, many claimed it was inspired by such a wall.

No one in their right mind would want to work there.

"I think you'll find it is not us," said Jester. "We're test-tube ladies, not builders."

"Way too busy," said Voted In Three.

❖

Beryl stood in the shed and, with her best "we are all in this together" look, said, "This could be the saving of us."

"Where have I heard that before?" said Voted In Two.

The door burst open. The market cleaner dropped her mile-high pile of boxes at her feet.

"They're wanting us to build a wall now," said Voted In One.

"Wall?" The market cleaner looked at Beryl. "Like in China?" She turned to her comrade. "But what about the fieldworkers? Won't they, you know, turn up—raid?"

"I have Mex taking care of that."

Jester and Nell stopped. They were almost impressed.

Bette was standing in the room with a view gazing out the window at her minions: women walking the street like they had somewhere to go and should have been there an hour ago.

How quickly things change, she thought.

At one time, the only thing a woman did in this room was clean; now they talked of revamping robots for such things.

"The women have brains," said Bigwig One. "Why not use them? Besides, a robot doesn't whine."

She stared at the designs on the table of a flexible male prototype with retractable arms and the ability to answer without sarcasm.

Funding that would set back her wall years . . .

"I thought we agreed to be more sustainable," she said.

Kate, idly flicking through the prototype design, didn't look up. In fact, no one did.

Once Bette mentioned "sustainable," there was no stopping her; a deaf ear was the only way to quell the onslaught.

A file drawer burst open with a robotic "tea?"

Another followed.

Cups clattered; napkins flew into the air.

The women sighed.

Kate blushed.

Bette, with a closed face, said nothing.

Installing the filing cabinets had been a piece of effluent, making the cabinets into weapons of mass destruction a breeze, but a beverage centre was *another pickling story all together, and quite frankly, she had had enough*.

Ten years of chaotic beverage breaks had worn Bette down. It was hard enough trying to rule a bunch of women who had an opinion on everything without an array of broken crockery to fund.

What was wrong with a good old fashion kettle?

The intercom light flashed red with a *beep*.

Bette, with an "what now" sigh, stared at the contraption, thinking about the possibilities of setting it on fire.

"It's the operations room," muttered a small voice.

Another drawer flew open. "Biscuits?"

"I know that," said Bette. "You *are* the only one connected to this thing."

"Oh, yes, forgot about the fire in the kitchen . . ."

"Make it quick," said Bette. "I can smell burning."

"Milk?" shouted the drawer.

"Is that tea on the go?" said the voice from the intercom.

"It's caffeine," snapped Bette.

Muffled noises came from the intercom . . .

"Teatime?"

"Caffeine, not tea."

"Forgot about that."

"Same thing."

"No, not really."

"I *said* . . . make it quick," snapped Bette.

"Oh, yes," said the voice from the intercom.

Bette, tight-lipped, waited as muffled talk came from the intercom.

"Get the kettle on."

"No, you."

"No, you—it's your turn."

"Pfff, *turn*—don't make me laugh."

"We can all hear you," yelled Bette.

"Oh, yes, meant to say: there's talk of riots in the gym," said the voice from the intercom.

"Riots?" said a voice from the back with a spray of biscuits.

"Well, more a revolt," said the voice from the intercom.

"*Strike!*" hissed a muffled voice.

"Sorry, I meant strike," said the voice from the intercom.

Kate looked up. "Strike, like on Earth?"

"Well, yes," said the voice from the intercom.

Bigwig One blew through her teeth. "A sticky situation."

Bette flashed a look at Bigwig One.

"Cream?" said a file drawer.

"*They're having cream,*" came the voice from the intercom.

"Ooh, lucky them," said another.

"We can all hear you," yelled Bette.

Legless, with a "shhhh," led his comrades to the gents', turned on the taps, and gestured for the others to commence flushing.

He looked about.

"We've five minutes."

"Five minutes for what?" said Manifesto the Great, ramming his wheelchair in the doorway.

The taps dribbled to a halt.

Legless gestured to John.

John threw a look at Jack.

Jack commenced flushing while Legless rattled off his speech on coercion, inside jobs, and his famed "foot in the door" theory.

"I want a revolt," yelled the ex-leader, "a Celtic charge, not some namby-pamby, jumped-up plan like your so-called beat-'em-at-their-own-game bollocks."

He huffed. "Whatever the pickle *that* is."

Silence . . .

Legless nodded to Jack.

Jack began the flushing again.

"Seduction is the way to go," whispered Legless. "There is nothing a joke and the flash of a decent leg can't sort with those women."

"Seduction?" said Mr Ex. "After a day's peddling, I can't even raise a spit, let alone anything else."

"Me neither," said Well Hung.

A few agreed.

Some nodded.

"Hear, hear," said Lumpy.

"Why have assets if you don't use them?" said Legless.

The men said nothing as Manifesto the Great attempted to reverse his wheelchair free of the doorframe.

A prolonged squeal of wheel on metal echoed through the gents'.

"Why must we always have meetings in this pickling john?" he snapped.

Mr Ex, spotting an uncomfortable rant brewing, pushed Manifesto the Great free and led him away from the toilets.

"You're a dreamer," yelled Manifesto the Great.

A few men coughed.

"You've the seduction techniques of a starfish."

Well Hung closed the door.

"Your stupid ideas have spread through the gyms quicker than a dose of salts."

"Shall I flush again?" muttered Jack.

"Best part of our day is laughing at you," yelled the ex-leader. "We all meet up on those wrist intercom things and have a great laugh," he lied.

"Shut it," muttered Mr Ex.

"I am prepared," Legless finally yelled back.

"You?" screeched the ex-leader. "You are as prepared for taking over as that Beryl is."

Legless looked at his comrades. "Trust me."

"Aye, but for what?" said the Guru as a toilet spontaneously flushed.

Chapter Twenty-One

WEAPONS AND TOSSING

"Being slow to act often gets quicker results."–Kate

*B*eryl stood at the top of the table in the room with a view, which was empty apart from Bette and a flashing intercom. She was seething.

She'd been summoned to solve the unsolvable, to save a mess not her making, and she was to do it with bugger-all budget and no recognition whatsoever.

"We have trouble brewing," said Bette.

"Your beverage centre?" said Beryl with a straight face.

"And you're to fix it."

"Fix it? What am I, a magician? What about the pickling wall?" said Beryl.

Bette wafted smoke from the intercom with a tut. "There will be no wall without a gym, will there?"

"Impossible," said Beryl. "I can't quell discontent on my own."

Bette huffed; her dreams for a wall were buggered if the men revolted.

She turned to Beryl. "Then get those prodigies to help. They do bugger-all."

"Prodigies aren't easy to manage," said Beryl.

"Manage? My girls have trained teenagers for all manner of things. What are yours doing? Cleaning Petri dishes? Sterilizing test tubes?"

"Bit more complicated than that," said Beryl.

"They did come up with the gym," came a voice from an intercom, followed by a puff of smoke.

❖

Beryl, pulling a fire blanket from a drawer, handed it to Bette.

Bette grabbed it. "Love to know what started it all."

"What?" said Beryl.

"The revolt," snapped Bette as she plopped the blanket over the intercom. "Why now?"

"Something to do with a book, ma'am," said the voice from the intercom.

"Rewritten history," said another.

Beryl blushed.

"What idiot rewrites history?"

"Victors?" mumbled Beryl.

Bette eyed Beryl like she knew why she was blushing, a trick she had learned years ago as a cleaner charging into a room with a "who left this pickling mess."

"You're to soothe, placate, and reason," said Bette.

"Good luck with that," came a voice from the fire blanket.

"And if that doesn't work, then threaten," said Bette.

"With what?" snapped Beryl.

"They're a shifty bunch, those men," *said* another voice from the intercom.

"That will be all," hissed Bette.

"Nothing gets by that Legless."

"I said that'll be all," yelled Bette.

Kate raced in, flushed. She had been searching all morning and finally found what she thought was her best innovation yet.

She thrust what looked like a wristwatch at Beryl, smiling. "My latest."

Beryl turned it in her hand.

"It's a portable intercom-thingy," said Kate.

Beryl looked at Kate.

"You can keep in contact."

"Oh," muttered Beryl. She gestured to the smoldering fire blanket. "Will I need one of those?"

Kate shook her head. Inspired by the dark side of Manifesto the Great, she designed all things with a dual purpose: with a toss, they could be used as a weapon in a fireball sort of way.

The only problem was, she never told anyone.

"As long as there is no tossing," she muttered.

Beryl, unconvinced, slid it onto her wrist.

A flame burst from the side of the fire blanket. Bette adjusted the blanket.

"Stabilization is the answer," said Kate.

Beryl looked confused.

"Use your initiative," said Bette.

Beryl headed for the door.

"And mind that Legless—don't let him get too close."

"I heard . . ." muttered Beryl.

"And Manifesto the Great," shouted Kate.

"I said I heard."

The door silently clicked behind her.

Bette turned to Kate. "What'd you give her that for?"

"Someone's got to test-run things," said Kate.

"That woman has our future in her hands and we are test-running?"

"She needs all the help she can get," said Kate. "That ex-leader never gives up."

"Exactly," said Bette, tossing water on the intercom.

Beryl stared into the back alley: the view from her bedroom. She still lived in the library, falling asleep to the rattle of water pipes and the scuttle of mechanical rats.

She dreamed of Bette's penthouse with a view, high up in the Building of Opulence; every day that dream seemed further away.

What did she know about strikes and persuasions?

When in doubt, spy, she told herself, heading to the operations room. If she timed it right, she could catch them at their break, or whatever the pickle it was called these days . . .

She slid into the room.. The kettle was on, and the Operators had gathered around it like a beacon of warmth.

"You pour."

"No, you."

"Shut it and have a biscuit."

"Biscuit? You could make a wardrobe out those things."

Beryl watched the "gym" monitor, expecting yelling, cursing, and all manner of male bonding. She was completely unprepared for a Legless in Lycra. He had lost his ostrich look.

"Give it some wellie," he shouted, erecting himself into a standing pedal.

Her heart skipped, her face flushed, her whole day forgotten as she stared at the sort of butt made for Lycra.

She tried to concentrate, focus. Not easy when Legless aroused feelings that she had never felt before, and in places she didn't know existed.

Beryl had grown up with a man in a wheelchair who wore wigs and coughed like a TB patient. Lycra was not something she was accustomed to, especially when covering a deliciously tight butt that clenched with each strut.

"You want a cup?" shouted Operator One from the kettle.

Beryl, tongue tied, shook her head.

"Biscuit?" said another.

Beryl said nothing; she was feeling weird. Sort of, well, girlie.

Operator Two plonked a mug beside her along with a rock-hard, month-old biscuit.

"It's only a butt," she said.

"Seen one, you've seen them all," said another.

Beryl sipped the insipid tea without a flash of disgust.

"But it's the only way to drink this effluent," laughed Operator One.

Beryl didn't even crack a smile, let alone laugh, but by the time she was on her second cup, she knew what she had to do.

Dare she?

Early the next morning, before dawn, Beryl slid into the dark and made her way to the room next to the gym.

It didn't take her long to find the peephole; there were peepholes everywhere, usually as well hidden as a light switch.

She peered into the gym, catching a whiff of male . . . something . . .

Legless was holding court, parading like a boxer in the ring, urging his "lads" to give their all "for the city."

It was Manifesto the Great who first saw her peering through the peephole. Poised by the rowing machine in his wheelchair, he caught Legless's eye.

"Keep shtum," mouthed Legless.

Not an easy thing to do for an angry man who had no idea what "shtum" was.

They cycled on for an hour . . . Legless, between puffs, talking of all they were lighting up.

"That'll be the canteen fueled, the institute set for the day . . ."

The men grunted.

"This town couldn't run without us."

"Hear, hear!" huffed a few.

Legless stood up to pedal again . . .

The men followed, pushing harder.

Manifesto the Great made grimacing faces at the peephole.

"Now for the sewage plant."

The men looked up. (The sewage plant recycled its' own energy).

"Just kidding," laughed Legless.

The men, sweating like boxers after twenty rounds, said nothing.

"Meant the streetlights," said Legless.

The men groaned.

Manifesto the Great swore.

Legless stopped.

"Or maybe not . . ."

He turned and flashed a look Beryl's way, like he knew she was there.

She stopped, gasping, as the face that had launched a dozen statues caught her eye.

Get a grip.

The men stopped; machines squealed to a halt.

Silence . . .

Legless strutted.

Beryl gulped.

He stopped near Manifesto the Great, lifted his Planet Hy Man's Geographic, and turned to the peephole.

"Shit," muttered Beryl.

"There'll be no more cycling today," shouted Legless like a preacher.

The men, with a cheer, flopped into their seats.

Chapter Twenty-Two

THE PORTABLE INTERCOM-THINGY

"The only thing men in the Art Centre were good for was the invention of a tracksuit or track-ie. It was even rumored by many that they introduced it to Earth . . ."–The Spark Plug Odyssey

"What's happening?" flashed on her intercom-thingy, lighting up the darkened room like the neon light of a strip joint.

"Shit and pickle!" hissed Beryl, covering the light.

"She's over there," mouthed Manifesto the Great, wheeling himself to the peephole.

The men sniggered.

Beryl swore. *Did they see the light?*

She took a chance . . . peered into the peephole . . .

The bloodshot eyeball of Manifesto the Great stared back.

It blinked.

Beryl jolted. *Shit . . .*

She pulled away, pressing her back flat against the wall . . .

It was early morning, and Bette couldn't sleep. She had a feeling in her waters, and when she stared into the streets and saw the lights waver, she knew her waters were right.

She flicked the kettle on—it was dead. Turned the radio on —silence.

Shit.

She looked at the portable intercom-thingy Kate had given her.

She jiggled it, pressed some buttons . . .

"Beryl!" she shouted. "Where are you?"

"Your caller is unavailable," said the portable intercom-thingy.

"What?" snapped Bette.

"Please leave a message."

"Message? I'm the leader. Leaders do not leave messages."

"Your call is important to us."

"I *am* the leader. Everything I do is important."

"Thank you for your message. Beryl will get back to you as soon as possible."

Bette stared at her wrist. "What is the pickling point of *you* if Beryl has *you* switched off?"

"Thank you for your message. Beryl will get back to you as soon as . . . possible."

Bette fumed. So much for testing, so much for keeping in contact.

"I may as well have strapped a cucumber to my wrist," she yelled.

"Thank you for your feedback. Your call is important to us."

Bette, tutting like there was no tomorrow, headed into the corridor.

She banged on Kate's door.

"It's happening," she shouted.

"What?" yelled Kate through her door.

"Gone tits up, blown up in our faces . . ."

"Tits up?" Kate yelled through her door.

"The revolt has started," said Bette.

Kate appeared, straighteners in hand, her hair like a bird's nest.

"A power cut is hardly a revolt," she snapped.

The lightbulb above Beryl's head flicked off; confusion flooded the street outside.

The early-morning workers, who had no idea of a luxury lie-in, were soon as agitated as a dog tied up in a butcher shop.

They were running late for work with a quota a mile long. A quota that had them racing to work every morning so early they drank their morning tea on the way.

Hungry, cold, and now in the dark, they had no idea how to get from A to B let alone work. They began to grumble.

They stared up at the Building of Opulence, clutching mugs of tea so rubbish it wouldn't even pass as dishwater.

"Where's the pickling lights?" boomed a woman.

"Yeah!" yelled another.

Beryl, hearing the women, jumped to her senses.

Legless climbed onto a table, pressing his face against the air vent, a slit so small he had to twist his head to position his lips at shouting angle.

"No more cycling till things are sorted," he spat.

The women looked about as the morning sun flashed onto the polished windows of the Building of Opulence and squinted.

Who said that?

Legless tossed a pellet of dried mechanical rat poo . . . he tossed another.

It hit the leg of a tall, thin woman who many called String Bean; she turned to see a flash of light through a vent illuminating a set of pearly white teeth and a cheesy grin.

"There'll be no more lights," spat Legless.

The women turned to the white teeth.

"Who the flying Petri dish are you?" snapped one.

"I represent the men," said Legless.

"You have representatives?" said a youngster.

Beryl heard it all; her hearing was so good she could hear a belch across a crowded room.

"Incoming messages," said the portable intercom-thingy.

Beryl pressed play.

The portable intercom-thingy lit up like a Christmas tree on Oxford Street.

"I *am* the leader. Everything I do—"

She pressed stop. Thinking on her feet, she raced upstairs using the light from her portable intercom-thingy.

Hearing voices in the room with a view, she opted for the "box" room next door, which was empty except for, well . . . boxes.

She stuck her head out of a window.

"Incoming messages," said the portable intercom-thingy.

Beryl flashed the light of her portable intercom-thingy on the main street below.

"I said there'll be no more cycling," yelled Legless.

"Cycling?" said String Bean. "I can't see where I am going let alone cycle."

"Yeah!" yelled the youngster.

❖

Bette was in the room with a view, a room with superb recycled triple glazing allowing little sound from outside. She had no idea of what was going on down below. All she knew was that the room with a view was now lit by candles and Kate, thanks to no straighteners, had the hairstyle of someone who had stuck their fingers into an electric socket.

Kate was trying to contact the other bigwigs—not an easy thing to do when the power was grinding to a halt.

"I've managed one," said Kate. "She is going to round up . . ."

She stopped.

Bette, with a maniac look, was in the process of trying to rip the "useless portable intercom-thingy" from her wrist. For some reason, anger had turned her fingers to thumbs.

For the last ten years, she had tried her best for this pickle-ridden city, always under the condescending look of know-it-all Beryl, and now that know-it-all bozo was unreachable . . .

"What's the point of *this*"—Bette glared at the intercom-thingy— "if it's switched off at the other pickling end?"

"Thank you for your message. You're next in the queue."

She made to toss.

Kate stopped her. "I wouldn't do that . . ."

Bette, retrieving her arm with a glare, snapped a "why not?"

"Because," hissed Kate.

"I have been on this thing all morning trying to contact that effluent of a woman, and will she answer? Now look at the place; the workers can't work and I can't have my toast."

"Your call is important to us."

A drawer burst open; napkins flew into the air.

"Iced tea, anyone?"

Kate tried to grab the portable intercom-thingy.

"Tossing . . ."

"Is too pickling good for it," snapped Bette.

She hurled it at the wall.

It burst into flames.

"And makes it flammable," muttered Kate.

Beryl could smell burning, feel something hot on her wrist . . .

She stared at her now-*smoking* portable intercom-thingy.

A small flame flickered.

"Shit!" hissed Beryl, ripping it from her arm.

She tossed it out the window.

Still panting, she stared at the expanding ball of flames hurling to the ground . . . straight toward the huddle of women.

They jumped.

It rolled onto the vent.

Legless flew from the table, swearing, as the now-melting portable intercom-thingy began to drip like volcanic lava into the gym.

"They're attacking," yelled one.

"Run away," yelled another.

"It's the Celts," screamed several.

"It's just a fire," yelled Legless, slapping the flames with a towel.

No one listened.

The gym emptied quicker than a quantum leap, only Mr Ex standing by. Manifesto the Great remained; his wheelchair had jammed at the first push.

The men stared at the now-burning table.

"That was quick," muttered Mr Ex.

The women in the street looked up, glowering at the Building of Opulence like it had personally ripped food from their bellies and burnt it in front of their noses.

Many working women spent time in the Art Centre and would have happily stayed if it weren't for the influx of men chased by the marauding fieldworkers. In fact, a growling fieldworker was the stuff of many women's nightmares.

Some blamed Bette and her lot for taking the herding all too far, for pushing them into the city, and for the rubbish jobs they now had.

They stared at the building.

"Who the Petri dish threw that?" yelled a red-faced woman.

The others strained their necks to see a ridiculous beehive of a hairdo disappear from view.

"Take that!" yelled a voice from the back, its owner hurling her tea.

A mechanical crow, caught in the crossfire, squawked.

Others followed, splashing the pristine windows of the Building of Opulence, some landing on the room with a view window near where that "stupid beehive" had appeared.

The city, now plunged into darkness, had a sense of panic about it, mainly because word of a fire had broken out—a firebomb sent by women to quell the strike.

It spread through the gym intercoms, setting off the sort of panic many would call "girlie."

The men had no plan B, let alone provisions for an attack. Legless had made out that an hour with no straighteners was enough to put those women in their place.

"Run," shouted many as they scattered like frightened sheep.

"Head for the hills," shouted others as they scurried like terrified rats.

Abandoning their gyms, they raced through the secret corridor like rabbits in a warren, ending up in a dark corner of the city with no idea where they were.

A mug crashed into the window of the room with a view.

Bette jumped. "What the sperm was that?"

"Hardly sperm," muttered Kate.

Bette opened the window and glared at the women.

"What's all this slinging about?" she shouted.

String Bean looked at her comrades. "Did she say 'slinging' or 'pinging'?"

"Slinging is too good for this tea," yelled a red-faced woman.

"It's so shit it's not even recyclable."

"Effluent's too good a word for it."

"Yeah!" yelled the youngster.

An even younger woman in orange appeared, barging into the crowd like she owned the place.

"Well, slinging is not the answer," she shouted.

"It works for me," said the red-faced woman with a toss of her mug.

Bette ducked as it sailed through her window and crashed against the side of a file cabinet. Lukewarm tea dribbled down the side and under its feet.

The cabinet sizzled . . .

Kate stopped, dipped her finger into the liquid. *Sugar?*

"There are better things to do with your time," said the woman in orange.

"What?" yelled Bette.

"I'm telling them there are better things to do with their time!" the woman in orange yelled.

"She's one of *them*," snapped String Bean.

"One of who?" said the youngster.

"Them!" said a voice from the back.

"Who is them?" said the woman in orange.

"Well, you would know, you're one of them," said the red-faced woman.

"What?" shouted Bette.

"One of you," shouted the youngster, tossing her mug.

Bette ducked again as a mug just shy of her head sailed through the window, landing with a crash on top of another file cabinet.

Piss-weak tea spilled over the top, dribbling into its drawers.

It sizzled, this time with a puff of smoke.

"Shit," muttered Kate.

Chapter Twenty-Three

THE BEEHIVE

"Democracy isn't the be-all and end-all."–Bette

Beryl, thinking on her feet yet again, raced down the stairs, charged into the street . . . and came face-to-face with a young woman sporting orange in various shades. She had the body of a weight lifter, the stance of a boxer, and the outfit of a drag act.

Inhaling the air of discontent, Beryl felt a surge of adrenaline. This was her time. This was what she was waiting for: a chance to take over.

"It's the beehive," said the youngster.

"Beehive?" said the woman in orange.

"Yeah, her from the window." String Bean turned to the woman in orange. "One of your lot."

"I'm no one's lot," snapped the woman in orange.

"Neither am I," said Beryl.

The women jostled with anger as Beryl plunged into her much-rehearsed "sisterhood" speech.

Beryl and her gigantic beehive were the last things they wanted to see. They were hungry, dying of thirst, seriously regretting the tossing of tea, and her being all fresh faced and eager really pissed them off. She had the polished look of someone who ate well, took hot baths, smothered her face in posh creams, and was hardly out of nappies. A mere teenager bounding out of the Building of Opulence like she owned the place, talking of pickling sisterhood.

"You can shove your sisterhood," shouted the youngster.

"But we could make a difference," said Beryl.

"Pfff—there's as much chance of that as a man landing on the moon," said String Bean.

Beryl, inspired by the great Winston Churchill, carried on: "Where there is hunger, I will feed; where there is shivering, I will hug."

"I'd rather a blanket," muttered a voice from the back.

"Or a cup of tea," snapped the youngster.

"On our own, we are but nothing . . ." said Beryl.

"Speak for yourself."

" . . . but together, we can move mountains."

"That's what my mother used to say," said the woman in orange.

Beryl stopped. "Your mother?"

"Fanny," said the woman in orange.

"Oh," muttered the other women. They shuffled uncomfortably.

"Yes, *that* Fanny, and she called me Verruca."

"Verruca?" said the women.

"Yes," said Verruca with a steely glare, daring them to laugh.

The women, taking in her muscular frame and shovel-like hands, nodded like it was the most normal name in the world to have.

Legless looked at his two comrades. "It's the chick with the beehive."

"Pfff—*her*."

"She's rustling up support."

"She couldn't rustle up an underwire, let alone support." The ex-leader chuckled at his wit.

"Sounds like they are listening," said Mr Ex.

"Bring her in here, let me work the old Legless magic."

Mr Ex rolled his eyes. What did he ever see in this Lycra-loving ponce?

Beryl talked of "sorting things." "Legless is the key," she proclaimed.

The youngster looked up at her tea splatted across the window. *What she wouldn't give for a sip now.*

"Him with the sock?" said String Bean.

"Sock?" said Beryl.

"Yeah, down his trousers."

"Used to see him prancing about the Art Centre," said the red-faced woman.

"Bit up himself—chopping wood's too good for him," said String Bean.

"There are statues of him all over the Art Centre," said the red-faced woman. "Totally ruined the place. It's enough to put you off your tea."

The youngster stopped. "He's the man in the statue?"

"Yes, but he's nothing like the statue," said String Bean.

"Oh." The youngster's face dropped.

Legless, unmoved by the sock comment, turned to Mr Ex.

"Now is the time," he said.

"What?"

"If I am the key to this situation, then we should let this Beryl turn it."

Manifesto the Great rolled his eyes.

❖

"Shhhh," hissed Verruca as the click of a walking stick echoed from the alley to the gym.

The women turned to see Mr Ex looking like he had lit a barbecue and run out of meat.

"He will see Beryl now," he sighed.

"*He'll* see *me?*" snapped Beryl. "It is I that will see him."

❖

Bette had to do something, *but what?*

She turned to Kate.

"You any good at cycling?"

Kate, in the middle of sourcing the sizzling in the file cabinet, looked up with a glower.

"Well someone's got to do it," snapped Bette.

"I am hardly going to light up a city with a few rounds on a bike, am I?" said Kate, pushing a drawer shut.

Bette paced the room. "Call the others."

"On what?" said Kate. "A megaphone?"

The door burst open; two of the bigwigs appeared clutching empty mugs and sporting the same bird's-nest hair as Kate.

"Don't any of you have a brush?" said Bette.

"What the pickle is going on?" said Bigwig One. "The streets are in darkness and tea's been hurled at my window like a bird with the runs."

Bette handed her a brush with a "here."

Kate grabbed it.

"I looked down," said Bigwig One, "and got abuse on par with those Celtic warrior women."

"Fieldworkers," said Bette with a blush.

"Yelling something about democracy," said Bigwig One.

"Oh, that," said Kate.

"What would workers know of democracy?" said Bigwig One.

"I heard the workers haven't turned up for their elevenses," said Bigwig Two.

"Just as well," said Kate. "There is nothing to heat things with."

"It's a strike," said Bette. She looked out the window.

The bigwigs stopped. "The women are on strike?"

"No, just the men. Although by the way things are going . . ." said Bette, catching an "up yours" gesture from the youngster.

"I thought Beryl was to fix things," said Bigwig Two.

Bette sighed. "So did I."

The women peered down to see the top of Beryl's beehive nodding in the middle of a huddle of women.

A woman in orange began to gesture toward the gym.

"Told you to be careful," said Kate.

"You did not," said Bette. "You just gave me that stupid listen-in thingy . . ." She sighed. "How can I think with no caffeine?"

"You used to," said Bigwig Two.

"Yes, well, 'used to' doesn't cut it," snapped Bette.

"I wonder what she's saying," said Kate.

"Least she doesn't need straighteners," grumbled Bigwig Two mid hair brushing.

Bette snatched the brush. "How can you brush at a time like this?"

"I am not facing a coup with bird's-nest hair," said Bigwig One.

Bigwig Two nudged her comrade. "Shut it."

Bette stopped.

"Coup?"

She turned to the women.

"What are we doing here? We need to stop them, sort them out before things overrun."

"Too late," said Kate. She gestured to the street. "They've disappeared."

The gym was empty apart from Legless casually oiling the wheel of Manifesto the Great's chair with the ex-leader still in it.

The ex-leader, engrossed, like he didn't trust Legless with such a mammoth task, pointed with a gnarled finger. "You missed a bit."

Beryl let out an "I'm here" cough.

"Where're the others?" shouted Verruca.

Legless, engrossed in polishing imaginary excess oil, was silent.

With a flick of a rag, he stood up. "That should do it, old man," he said like he was looking for a tip.

"Less of the 'old,'" said Manifesto the Great.

Verruca grew impatient.

She nudged Beryl.

Beryl stuttered. "I've come to offer you an olive branch."

"Pfff—what do we want with a branch?"

"Yeah, a branch—what's that when it's at home?" snapped Manifesto the Great, sparking off a coughing fit.

"Figure of speech," said Verruca, "as well you know."

Legless, with a grin, thrust a cup under the ex-leader's chin. "Spit it out, old man."

"I said less of the 'old,'" spat the ex-leader.

"He's cocksure of himself," whispered Verruca.

Beryl didn't hear; her heart was pounding.

Legless had the sort of square hands that looked equally at home massaging as chopping wood.

With an expert flick of his rag, Legless wiped the chin of the ex-leader, then caught Beryl's eye.

Verruca snatched his cloth. "And you can cut the act. This man's coughing is as convincing as your pickling sock."

Legless mounted his bike.

A small fart squeaked from his Lycra.

Beryl tried not to stare, not to think of what was underneath. *Focus on the fart,* she told herself. Not easy when Legless was astride his bike like it was a wild stallion.

Beryl gulped. Legless's long nose and dark lips had her as spellbound as the sock beneath his trousers did.

He eyed her, moved his hips about the saddle, and adjusted his sock.

She blushed.

"Nice beehive," he said, winking.

"All right, that's enough," said Verruca, "give the seduction a rest."

"I don't know what you mean," said Legless.

"Just put your sock back in its drawer and tell us where the others are," said Verruca.

Legless turned to Beryl. "Really do like your beehive. Dark suits you."

"We're not here to talk of beehives," said Verruca.

Legless glanced from one woman to the other. "So that's how you want to play it? Good Voted In–Bad Voted In?"

"There is nothing playful about us," said Verruca.

He caught Beryl's blush.

"Ladies, I beg to differ."

Chapter Twenty-Four

FAIRY TALES

"Spying is the foreplay of war."–Planet Hy Man's National Geographic

It was Verruca who first noticed Manifesto the Great's book; she lifted it with a "what is this?"

"Exactly," snapped Manifesto the Great, "and you, Beryl, should be ashamed of yourself."

Beryl attempted to grab the book, forgetting how heavy it was.

"That's right, snatch away your lies," he huffed.

"They are not lies," said Beryl.

She stumbled.

Legless caught her.

The book fell to the floor, opening to the infamous "Beryl" chapter.

Beryl stared at the blacked-out words and the scribbled comments.

"Fairy tales, four-legged-fantasy shit," he said.

"What did you expect, a eulogy?" snapped Beryl.

Legless lifted the book like it was a leaflet. He caught Beryl's eye and held it . . .

"It is a bit far-fetched," he said with a blank face.

Beryl huffed. "History is written by the victors."

Verruca, with a suspicious glance at Beryl, snatched the book from Legless.

Her mother had warned her of women like Beryl: stuck up so-and-sos with stupid hairstyles.

She opened the book . . .

"Blimey," she muttered.

She flicked a page.

"The Librarian—a woman?"

"He was as good as one," said Beryl. "I saw the wigs."

"Told you, four-legged shit," snapped Manifesto the Great.

"What would you know?" said Beryl. "You were so high on cocktails and meat."

Verruca turned a page.

"You really went to town . . . it's like a different city." She tutted. "Even my mother would be ashamed of this."

The red-faced woman, the youngster, and String Bean watched in the alleyway by the gym entrance waiting for that *damnable* Beryl.

No one saw them.

A young man climbed out a trapdoor in the pavement, followed by an elderly gent.

A dark man ran past, bumping into the elderly gent.

"Run away!" he yelled.

The elderly gent scratched his head, dazed.

"To the hedge," yelled the dark man.

"But what about those women—the Celts?" said the elderly man.

The young man looked from one to the other like he was stoned. "Celts?"

"Split up," said the dark man. "Meet at the quarry, I know a secret entrance."

"Another?" said the young man, looking at the trapdoor. "Does it lead anywhere?"

The two men eyed the young man like he was a Martian of epic stupidity and argued over who to take him.

"You."

"No, you."

The Guru sprinted by and stopped.

The dark man and the elderly gent took one look at the spindly legs and scattered. Making it to the quarry with him aboard was as likely as his loincloth remaining in place.

The women stared; male flesh was as foreign to them as a good cup of caffeine.

The young man, watching the two men disappear with a glazed "what have I done" look, blinked.

"You've been on the hemp?" snapped the Guru.

"No," lied the young man.

"The last thing you need to be is high when there's a coup in *situ*."

The red-faced woman looked at her comrades and mouthed, *Coup?*

"I know nothing of a coup," said the young man. "Or a *sit-you*, for that matter. But I do know where I can get some trousers."

"Trousers? How can you speak of trousers at a time like this?"

"How can you speak of sitting in that getup?" said the young man.

The Guru eyed the young man's blank face. "You're not really a full cup of tea, are you?"

The young man blinked, confused.

"You know—not batting with a full team."

"I don't play sports," said the young man.

"Never mind," muttered the Guru. "We need to find a place to hide."

"They are heading for the quarry," said the young man. "Apparently, there's a secret entrance."

❖

The red-faced woman pulled her two comrades to the entrance of the gym.

"We are in the middle of a coup."

"What's that when it's at home?" said the youngster.

"Shhhh," said String Bean. She pressed her ear to the door.

❖

Manifesto the Great stopped and looked to the door. He could hear voices . . .

"Shhhh . . .

"You shhhh."

"Shut it, they'll hear."

Manifesto the Great turned to Mr Ex. "They're coming—we need to get out of here."

"In that thing?" said Verruca. "That chair is as convincing as Legless's sock."

Legless, ignoring the "sock" comment, did his best to saunter to the door.

"Don't," hissed Manifesto the Great. "They'll tear us to pieces."

"That's ridiculous," said Mr Ex. "They are hardly going to attack an old man in a wheelchair."

Legless yanked opened the door.

Three women, mid ear wigging and way too young to remember free men, jumped.

They took in the gym and the grumpy-looking git in a wheelchair and quickly pulled themselves together.

"Where did those women go?" said Bette with restrained panic.

"The gym, by the looks of it," said Kate.

"What will they do there?" said Bette.

"Try to run things, I imagine," said Bigwig One.

She stopped; Bette looked panicky.

"Run things? But I run things," said Bette.

Bigwig One patted her shoulder. "You're still the leader."

"That Beryl will turn the men. Take over."

"The men are old," said Bigwig Two.

"Ancient," said Bigwig One.

"Anarchy," Bette mumbled to herself.

Kate watched as the men silently charged down the street like startled rabbits.

"Where's the fire?" she said.

Bette stopped. "Fire?"

"There's no fire," said Bigwig Two with a patronizing look at her leader.

Bigwig One joined Kate. "Blimey, they can move."

She caught Bette's crazed look. "For old gits."

"Gits? What gits?" said Bette, verging on hysterical.

"We have the hedge. They'll hardly get past that," Kate said to Bigwig One.

"Hedge?" screeched Bette.

"Calm down," soothed Bigwig Two with a "tone it down" glare at her comrades.

"That thing is hardly a hedge. We may as well open a gate and give them a transporter."

"And if that don't stop 'em," said Kate, "the fieldworkers will."

Bette glowered. "Don't even mention that word to me." She looked at the window. "What's going on out there?"

"Nothing," said Kate and Bigwig One together.

Bette moved to the window.

"I wouldn't look out there," said Bigwig One.

"Yes, let's have a nice cup of caffeine," said Bigwig Two, taking Bette by the arm.

"Iced?"

"Anarchy," Bette muttered again. "And I'll be blamed."

A string of men disappeared around the corner.

"Now that's what I call running," said Bigwig Two.

Bette jolted, spilling her iced beverage.

"Running? Who's running?"

"They can't get far," muttered Kate, catching sight of the Guru, who, clutching his loincloth, was sprinting by with surprising speed.

Chapter Twenty-Five

WAR CRY

"Tongue-poking is an art lost on a turtle."–Mex

"Come in," said Legless with an exaggerated bow.

"We don't need to be invited," said the red-faced woman, entering.

The other two followed, sniffing; there was more than a whiff of male sweat, and they had never been near a man, let alone smelt one.

The youngster caught sight of Legless; he looked like his statue. In fact, he looked way better.

He smiled.

She jiggled the handlebar of a bike. "So this is where it all happens."

"Try it," said Legless.

String Bean woman threw her a "don't" look.

Feet pattered over the grill on the ceiling.

"Get him!" yelled a woman from above.

A male shrieked.

❖

"They're heading for the hedge," said the youngster, sliding onto the bike.

The red-faced woman threw her a "get off" look.

"Via the quarry," said the youngster, making herself comfortable.

"How would you know?" said Manifesto the Great.

The youngster eyed Legless. "I heard."

"As if," said the ex-leader.

"Did too." She looked at her comrades. "Didn't we?"

They said nothing, not quite sure who to trust.

"Even a man in a loincloth is heading there," she said.

The men jumped. *Loincloth?*

"And how would you know?" said Beryl.

"Just do." She shrugged.

She slid off the bike and sauntered to the water cooler.

"They were all running about like headless birds, no idea of what to do, until *he* came along," she lied.

"Shut it," hissed the red-faced woman.

The youngster moved to the headless obelisk.

"What's this?"

"That's mine," shouted the ex-leader.

"All right, keep your Lycra on," the youngster laughed.

No one said anything.

The youngster's flirting had taken the others by surprise—apart from Legless, who was lapping it up like a sex-starved soldier back from the front.

The cooler spluttered a few drops.

"I'm gagging for a drink," she said.

"Here, let me," said Legless with a strut.

Mr Ex huffed.

Beryl bristled.

"I can do it," giggled the youngster.

"Oh, for galaxy's sake," snapped Verruca.

Another male shrieked, this time not from above but from somewhere in the room.

"What was that?" said Verruca.

"Nothing," said the men in unison.

"Something about *tits up?*" said String Bean.

Manifesto the Great reversed toward the obelisk. "I didn't hear a thing."

The red-faced woman gestured to the obelisk. "It's coming from there."

"I said that's mine," snapped Manifesto the Great.

"Trust me, it's nothing," blurted Legless.

"Run for your lives," squeaked a voice from the obelisk.

"Where's that voice coming from?" The red-faced woman rattled the water cooler. "Here?"

Legless and Mr Ex made to stop her.

"Or from this?" She lifted the obelisk.

"Here, what do you think you're doing?" yelled Manifesto the Great.

He grabbed the obelisk; they tussled.

"*No!*" shouted Legless and Mr Ex.

The red-faced woman clung on with a vigor that took her by surprise.

The obelisk cracked.

Manifesto the Great, his fingers glued to the base, didn't let go.

She pulled, staggered, then tripped with the top of the obelisk firmly in her hands.

The obelisk cracked like an egg, and just like an egg, its innards spilled onto the ground.

The women stared at the egg box.

"It's nothing," said Mr Ex.

"An egg box is never nothing," muttered Beryl.

She pulled it open: two portable intercom-thingy's and the motherboard.

"Just a couple of watches," said Mr Ex.

Verruca picked up the mother connection.

"And an egg timer."

"Run away!" squeaked a voice.

"Shit," muttered Mr Ex.

Beryl slid on a portable intercom-thingy. I*t had the look of a Kate invention.*

She turned the other in her hand as Verruca tuned the mother connection to the operations room.

Beryl listened to the women . . . and a plan hit her.

A plan that needed the men silenced, tied up, and out of action . . .

"Get some rope."

The women stopped.

"You heard: tie them up. There must be some rope somewhere."

"Even the ex-leader?" said Verruca.

Beryl nodded.

"You want to tie up an old man?"

"Here, less of the 'old,'" snapped Manifesto the Great.

"He's in a wheelchair, he's hardly going anywhere," said String Bean.

Beryl gestured to Legless. "Start with him."

The youngster jumped. "I'll do it."

Beryl almost smiled.

What they needed now was a good kicker, a fighter with no fear, and perhaps a whip.

Manifesto the Great eyed her back. "You should be ashamed of yourself."

"So you keep saying," she said, then stopped.

"Mex," she said quietly. "Now there's a woman who could lasso a man."

"Lasso?" grumbled the ex-leader. "Why the sperm would you want to do that?"

Beryl thrust the portable intercom-thingy at Verruca with a "here, you're gonna need this."

Verruca threw her a look.

"Just don't, whatever you do, throw it—unless, that is, you're in the mood for a good run."

Verruca sighed. She had a bad feeling in her waters.

A few hours later, Mex was at the quarry following instructions while kicking things.

She had been told to "watch for men" by some weird woman in orange called Verruca, who Beryl had apparently sent . . .

What next?

❖

It seemed ages since Mex had been dragged from her bunk bed and listened to Beryl's plans to take over . . . and it had not been easy.

Making an army out of knee-high robotic turtles was as easy as picking up an egg yolk with your fingers.

Lining up was a nightmare; a mere sniff of something organic had the turtles either rearing on their hind legs like stallions or retreating into their shells.

Unity was not their strength. They were as individual as a bunch of immigrants speaking different languages. In fact, she sometimes wondered if they did.

Mex did her best, making the most of their saber tooth teeth. She sat the turtles in front of reruns of Earth rugby matches to watch the Maori haka.

"Now that's a war cry," she said with a flick of the remote.

The turtles, unmoved, blinked . . .

"ARRRRRR!" screamed Mex, scaring half into their shell.

The others, attempting to follow, stuck their tongues out like they were licking ice cream.

It was work in progress . . .

❖

Mex was in the quarry marching through her turtle lines the day the men escaped.

She'd spent all morning teaching a bite-on-command move, reinforced with a crouch and diagonal lunge, and hoped to move on to the propelling of robotic appendages after lunch.

She was pleased with her team, and she was talking of a run through the haka when Verruca appeared with what she called "an enhanced army plan."

Namely attacking men *as well* and moving forward the starting date from a month away to pretty much anytime soon.

"That's impossible," said Mex.

Verruca looked at the turtles moving into their haka stance.

"Not now," said Mex.

They began to chant, working on their lion faces . . .

"I said not now."

"Arrrgh!" yelled some; others looked confused.

"At ease," yelled Mex. She turned to Verruca. "Needs some tweaking."

Verruca nodded.

"Beryl said you'd know what to do."

Mex stopped. "She said that?"

"'I have absolute faith in my kicker,' she said."

Mex, red-faced and too flustered for a comment, picked up the ball and socket of a Mae West prototype's knee. She balanced the joint in her hand, tugging at the legion of tubes and wires sprouting from it, then landed it at the feet of a turtle with a playful kick.

A turtle kicked it back.

Verruca looked at the "at ease" turtles lounging about the quarry while sucking and flicking hemp rollups like First World War soldiers. Their wrinkled, world-weary faces looked older than Wifie-ie's obelisk.

"Are they allowed to smoke?" said Verruca.

"You try getting a turtle to dive and roll without a little incentive," snapped Mex.

A turtle pulled a haka face at Verruca with an "arrrgh."

Verruca jumped. The last thing he looked like he was doing was licking ice cream.

❖

Beryl, her head finally taking over her heart, looked around at the gym. They needed to move.

"You, get me a flashlight—let's really put the wind up those so-called bigwigs."

"You're flashing code red?" said Mr Ex.

"And what if I am?" said Beryl.

"It'll send them into a panic. They'll think we've taken over," said Mr Ex.

Beryl smiled. "Exactly."

Kate stopped, catching sight of the flashing light from the ceiling window of the gym.

"They are flashing code red," she said.

"The men are flashing?" said Bette.

"How?" said Bigwig One.

"They'll take over," Bette said to herself. "They'll have me strung up, out, and inside like one of those mechanical . . . what do you call 'em?"

"Not the men, you idiot, it's *Beryl*," said Kate.

"Beryl?" yelled Bette. She charged to the window. "How do you know?"

"She's using your code!"

Bette stopped. "Oh, god of galaxies, that's even worse."

"Try to keep calm," said Kate.

"Beryl will rule," shrieked Bette.

The bigwigs looked at each other. *Her with that beehive?*

"She'll make me clean again," said Bette. "String me up."

"No one's stringing anyone up," said Kate.

"I'm not cut out for this," wailed Bette.

Kate shook her. "Get ahold of yourself. Where's that cleaner who ransacked the locker rooms?"

"Where's my mop?" said Bette.

"You want that beehive to take our suits, our penthouses?"

"Bring me my bucket!" shouted Bette.

Kate shook her again. "Get ahold of yourself."

"Give her here," snapped Bigwig One.

"Get ahold of yourself," she said with a slap.

"Anarchy," mumbled Bette.

"Pull yourself together!"

"Pure anarchy," Bette muttered.

"Think, damn you, think!" shouted Bigwig One.

Bette flopped into a chair.

"Run," she muttered.

Chapter Twenty-Six

THE OPERATIONS ROOM

"Running away is all a man is good for."—A fieldworker

The Guru sprinted toward the quarry at a speed that had the young man panting with surprise.

He ran with the stamina of a marathon runner approaching the finish line and no fear of being seen. Twice the young man had to pull him behind a bush.

The Guru was excited. He had heard of a hippie colony in the outlands, and they were *this* close . . . all they had to do was make it past those wild women of the fields.

"Come on," yelled the Guru. "We might be able to make it to the hedge before those Celts wake up."

"Celts?" said the young man.

"Fieldworkers," said the Guru.

"Oh, them. They'll be up by now. Best bring them something; they like nice soap."

The Guru stopped with a "how do you know?"

"I trade with 'em," said the young man. "Where do you think I get the hemp?"

He eyed the young man, who now appeared sober, and nodded.

"Incoming! Incoming!" shouted a circling turtle.

Mex looked at Verruca. "The men are coming . . ."

"What's a man anyway?" said the turtle known as the Captain.

"Yeah," said another with a flick of his stub.

"A mere git with dangly bits," said the Captain, "hardly panic material. A few hakas and they'll be running like Jessies."

Mex and Verruca looked up to see the Guru sprinting along the top of the quarry followed by a young man clutching trousers.

"Incoming! Incoming!"

The Guru stopped. "What was that?"

"Oh, that. That's just a turtle."

"With those teeth?"

"They just need some friendly persuasion. Seen them about the hedge; apparently they like ice cream," said the young man, attempting a chin-tickle.

A robotic head sailed through the air like a missile as the turtle snapped at his fingers.

He ducked, catching sight of a muscular woman taking aim—again.

"Watch out," hissed the young man.

The Guru stood up with a "what?"

Mex kicked a Mae West knee socket; it sailed through the air, its wiry attachments flapping like a Rastafarian's dreadlocks.

"Duck!" shouted the young man.

The Guru looked at him.

The socket hit his head.

The Guru yelled.

The socket clattered to the ground.

The Guru, rubbing his head, glowered at the mass of wires and tubes.

"What the loincloth was that?"

The young man peered over the ledge again.

Mex, clutching another robotic head, was rounding up the turtles, who appeared to be licking air while tossing hemp cigarette stubs to the wind.

He pulled the Guru to the ground . . .

A Mae West head shot past the Guru just shy of his beard.

The two men peered over the ledge.

Mex, her dark janitor coat flapping like a cape, was scaling up the quarry with the ease of a mountain goat.

The Guru was transfixed.

She moved with impressive speed, like a wrestler made of muscle.

"Come on!" she shouted to the turtles below.

"You heard her: war cry!" shouted Captain.

The young man grabbed the Guru.

"Let's go."

Mex stopped, catching sight of Guru's loincloth.

"You wearing a hanky?" she yelled.

"Grrrrrrrr!" shouted the turtles.

"Hanky?" yelled the Guru. "This ain't no hanky."

"Looks like one," she shouted.

"It's a pickling loincloth."

"Loincloth? For what—polishing?"

The young man began to panic.

Mex, clutching robotic appendages like they were socks, was looming closer.

"Grrrrrrrr!" shouted the turtles.

"How dare you?" shouted the Guru.

The young man tugged the Guru's arm. "Come *on*!"

"She's insulting my loincloth, my spiritual coverings." The Guru pulled a boxer stance. "She needs a good seeing to, a good punch."

The young man eyed the Guru's chicken-leg arms. "We need to run."

"Run? From her? I'm gonna knock her block off."

"With those arms? You couldn't knock a toilet roll. Now come on," said the young man. "They'll be here any minute, and by the looks of things, she's more—*shit!*"

He pulled the Guru to the ground.

A Mae West prototype foot flew past, landing inches from the Guru's foot.

He stopped, touching the painted toenail, the curved ankle, his foggy memory clearing to precision.

Memories of happy years of Mae West prototype back rubs flooded back.

He charged down the quarry, meeting Mex halfway.

Up close, she looked younger.

The Guru took in her teenage skin and thought, *A piece of effluent.*

Mex, who had no idea of age, let alone beards, was completely unprepared for any feelings. She had been told not to trust men. But when she looked into the leathery face, the map of wrinkles, the shivering, stick-thin limbs, she felt something strange . . .

Was it sympathy?

The Guru, catching sight of a beloved Mae West prototype head swinging from Mex's hand, knew what he felt—rage.

He snapped. "Is there no end to your torment?"

"What?" said Mex, her face almost soft.

The Guru, with no thought of her soft face, sprang into action.

A Mae West prototype foot flew past, landing inches from the

Bette was standing in the operations room. It was Kate's idea.

"Just watch," she said. "Perhaps something will hit that brain of yours."

Bette stared at the screens. There were several, all focused on different parts of the city. Her eyes flashed from screen to screen with a look of glazed confusion.

"You want the gym?" said a small Operator.

Bette blinked at the Operator known as Knee-High.

She was so short she needed a stool on top of a chair to see the screen.

"'Cause I can give you the gym," said Knee-High, "if that's what you want."

"Don't confuse her," said Kate.

"Confuse our leader?" said Knee-High.

Bette glanced at Knee-High.

"Do I know you?" she said with a vague interest in the answer.

"Well, no—but you knew my father."

Bette stopped. "You have a father?"

"How do you think I ended up this size? In a Petri dish?"

"Don't listen to her, she wants someone to blame," said Operator Two.

"You're not from a Petri dish?" said Bette.

Knee-High, mid tuning her screen, stopped.

"Apparently, I am the happy accident of a malfunctioning mop and way too much hemp."

"A male white coat," said Operator Two. "Caught off guard, celebrating—so the cleaner says."

"I mean look at this," huffed Knee-High. She reached for the sky. "A snail has better reach than me."

"Never celebrate in a laboratory," said Bigwig One. "Skews the measurements."

"Too right," said Operator Two.

Kate threw a look at Bigwig One. "How would you know?"

She shrugged. "I've heard things—been around."

"Yeah, like that cleaner," said Operator Two. "A malfunctioning mop—as if."

"Can't even reach for my cup," muttered Knee-High.

"Let's focus," said Kate.

"When you say 'not a Petri dish' . . . do you mean the old-fashioned way?" said Bette.

"Jack was celebrating a new shortcut for fertilizing," said Operator Two, "when *she* appeared. 'My mop needs mending,' *she* says, like she couldn't screw a head on herself."

"Jack?" said Bette, sparking to life.

"Did more than screw a head on, I can tell you. Everyone heard them," said Operator Two. "Got so carried away they buggered up the fermenting process."

"Jack and a cleaner? Impossible," said Bette.

"Instead of a Petri dish, Knee-High ended up in one of those long glass tubes," said Operator Two.

"A cleaner, with Jack?" Bette shook her head.

"All scrunched up like a used condom—no room to expand."

"Jack never expanded in *my* day," muttered Bette.

"Test tubes?" said Bigwig One. "She was made in a test tube?"

"Don't mention test tubes around her," said Operator Two.

"Test tubes ruined my life!" yelled Knee-High. "I am as disabled as a headless robot."

Kate rolled her eyes, then nodded to Operator Two.

"Tune to the main gym."

❖

Legless flashed on screen one.

❖

The youngster was tying Legless's hands behind his back while Legless was raging like an anarchist on coke.

"Things are afoot," he yelled. "And we men are part of that foot."

The youngster pulled a knot.

"We have demands, needs—we are more than a pair of legs."

"Tighter," said Beryl.

Legless turned to Beryl.

"We are nothing but cyclists to you."

"I said tighter."

"We are flesh and blood—" Legless grunted. "Ow! Cut me, do I not bleed? . . . Ouch!"

"You've been watching too much Earth," said the red-faced woman.

Legless began to tussle. "We have rights, strategies, links, networks even!" he yelled.

The youngster grabbed him.

The others charged to follow.

A bike crashed to the ground; its pedal swung to a halt.

❖

"I'd need a ladder to get on one of those rowing machines, let alone a bike," muttered Knee-High.

"What would be the point?" hissed Bigwig One. "You couldn't reach the pedals."

Knee-High huffed.

"Tune to the quarry," snapped Kate.

❖

The quarry flashed on screen two. The Guru threw a punch at Mex; she ducked, slipping on the remains of a Mae West prototype wig.

The Guru, ignoring the young man's "come on" tug, dove like a stunt man.

They rolled. For a moment, his loincloth looked dangerously loose . . . until they disappeared off the ledge, leaving the loincloth behind.

❖

"He looks the sort you wouldn't want to rub up the wrong way," cackled Bette.

"Let's just stick to the crisis," said Kate.

"Not that I am into rubbing," laughed Bette with a crazed look.

The women glared at Bette like she was an idiot.

"Rubbing is the last thing to do to a man," snapped Operator Two.

"Now look at me—no one sees me," Knee-High muttered to herself.

"Poor you." Bette ruffled her hair. "Poor teeny, knee-high, baby you. You're like a little Twinkie."

Kate threw Bette a look.

"I can go anywhere—incognito as a puff of wind," said Knee-High.

Kate stopped. "Anywhere?"

"Why, yes," said Knee-High.

"Let's tune to the hedge," said Kate.

Screen three tuned to the hedge, a higgledy-piggledy line of wild-looking shrubs—tatty, brown, and covered in fieldworker washing.

(The Operators could tell from the scratchy look of the material.)

The men running toward the hedge slowed down with a confused look.

A sheet flapped in the wind, revealing a motley collection of socks and flannels.

"Laundry?" mouthed one.

"What shall we do?" panicked another.

"Shhhh," hissed many.

No one saw the fieldworkers, not even the Operators, until their painted faces jumped from beneath the sheets screaming like football fans; socks scattered and flannels flew high.

The men stopped.

"Pussies!"

"Jessies!"

"Real meat!" yelled the fieldworkers.

The men, screaming like terrorized rats, ran while the fieldworkers collapsed in laughter.

"Impressive war cry," muttered Bette.

Kate sighed.

Chapter Twenty-Seven

THE WRONG SIDE OF THE TRACK

"The sock mystery was over before it started."—A Footman's Diary

"Have you been to the hedge?" said Bette.

"Loads of times," lied Knee-High.

She had been to the quarry once, years ago, when she was ten and eager to be part of "the gang."

It was the first time she'd clapped eyes on a prodigy, and it was the first time Mex had seen a girl outside the laboratory.

Knee-High and the gang came from "the wrong side of the tracks," the complete opposite from a prodigy; there were no privileges.

Seeing Mex set off a tirade of bullying that Knee-High chose to forget. There were ten of them and one Mex; some say it was the making of Mex.

"There are places you can hide in for days," muttered Knee-High. "I've seen them all." She stopped. "On my days off."

"You have days off?" said Bigwig One.

"Of course they have days off," said Bette.

She turned to Knee-High. "Would you like one now?"

"Tea?" said a young cleaner standing in the doorway.

Bette stared at the cleaner her uniform looked familiar.

"Didn't you used to work in the institute?"

"I may have," said the young cleaner.

Jack, running from the hedge, appeared on screen three.

The cleaner blushed "sugar?'
Knee-High glared with a "you can shove your tea" look.

The cleaner parked her tray and with a red face left.

Bette detected an atmosphere.
"What's her name?"
"Hilda," spat Knee-High.
"You know the name of your cleaner?" said Bigwig One.
"Everyone knows Hilda." Operator Two coughed uncomfortably.
"Knowing names is all part of their democratic rights," said Bette.
Operator Two glanced at Knee-High. "Despite what they apparently get up to."

Hilda headed out, making her way to the cleaner's beverage hub, which was more a bench than a hub.
Her mate looked up and handed her a mug. "I take it that Knee-High was there."
"Isn't she always?
Hilda grabbed her mug, "but who cares
revolution is afoot."
"Oh," said Vegas.
"Looks like you were right."

Vegas nodded. "Now all we have to do is choose the right side."

Hilda nodded. "Absolutely."

❖

Beryl looked up from the intercom. *So Bette's moved to the operations room.*

That place could see everywhere.

She wondered what to do, where to go. It had all happened so fast . . .

She eyed Legless astride a seat. Despite being tied up, he looked like he was, well, having fun.

Then it hit her . . . the cabinets.

"Take the men to the room with a view."

The women looked up with a startled "what?"

"Are you mad?" said the red-faced woman.

"Trust me," she said.

"Let's start with Mr Socks over there."

Legless mocked a head bow.

"Him?" said String Bean. "He's always got something up his sleeve."

"Exactly," said Beryl.

"Not to be trusted."

"Too right," said Beryl.

"I'll do it," the youngster jumped in.

❖

Hilda and Vegas watched as Knee-High left the Operator's room.

"She'll never forgive," said Vegas.

"Who cares," lied Hilda.

"She'll always hold you responsible."

"Pfff." Hilda shrugged. "I've better things to think of. It's not my fault she's an idiot—like that Jack. He's probably heading for the quarry as we speak, like that is going to help him."

She sighed.

Vegas nodded. Lies oozed out of Hilda like treacle. No one could detect them apart from her, but then she had grown up with Hilda.

Cleaners came from "the wrong side of the track," out-of-the-way compounds that fed little girls on a diet of watery porridge and "serving the planet is its own reward" bollocks.

The compounds, run by nannies (or nans as the girls called them), trained girls to be doers of dirty work, and the nans had quotas to fill.

Quotas with no room for rejects.

The girls had the privileges of prisoners. They were taught to work, told "button it," and punished with extra cleaning duties for asking questions—usually a nan's shoes or other "unmentionables."

The restrictions were so tight that many girls went crazy when they left. Dining out on hemp "whatever," eyeing up what was left of men, and indulging in the sort of "dangly bit" jokes that could turn a man impotent.

Some men saw their removal to the gym a blessing.

It was not unusual for a man to be catcalled in the street when herded to a gym or for the likes of those left to pass on knowledge to be touched, jeered, and taunted.

In fact, it was just such taunting that sent Jack into overdrive—proving that his dangly bit did way more than merely dangle.

Hilda often wondered, after a night on the hemp, if the power of such an appendage could be harnessed.

"It is a sight to behold," she often said to Vegas. The only "Hilda" comment Vegas didn't question; an appendage to her was as foreign as Parmesan cheese.

Hilda believed in spying and coercion, although even she would admit she took the whole coercion thing too far with Jack. The truth was, she was young and ill prepared for the feelings a man in a white coat and glasses would rise in her.

Facing such a debacle as Knee-High head on took a heart of steel, and where that heart of steel was heading, Vegas was going too.

"We're heading for something higher," said Hilda. "Just need that Knee-High out of the way."

Vegas never asked what "out of the way" meant, any more than what that "something higher" was. Hilda was better a friend than a foe.

"We should follow," said Hilda. "This could be our chance."

"But they'll notice, won't they?"

Hilda smiled. "Not if I'm on trolley-squeaking duty."

The youngster and the red-faced woman took Legless to the room with a view.

The youngster sat him on the chair.

"You're nothing without us," he said.

"So you say," snapped the red-faced woman.

"Take straighteners for a start," said Legless.

"I don't use them," said the youngster with pride.

"Well, you will one day."

"Pfff—as if. Straighteners are for bigwigs," said the red-faced woman. She tossed a rope at the youngster. "Tie him up and don't listen to him. He's as silver tongued as those Earth leaders."

"Why should the bigwigs have all the straighteners?" Legless eyed the youngster.

She blushed.

"I told you, don't listen to him," said the red-faced woman. She pulled his arms around the back of the chair. "Now tie him up."

"You'll not stay young forever," Legless whispered to the youngster. "One day you'll wake to a bird's nest like the rest, and then you'll need me—us, our power."

"I am happy with a brush," she stuttered.

Mr Ex, his hands already bound behind his back, burst through the door, pushed in by String Bean.

He staggered to his feet, catching a side glance at his comrade on a chair with the youngster tying his feet.

"Tighter," hissed the red-faced woman.

"If you just kept that sock and sauntering in order, we wouldn't be in this predicament," he yelled.

He stopped—the file cabinets. He'd *forgotten about them*.

String Bean pushed him onto a chair and began to tie.

"Well, this has changed." He winced.

"Changed how?" said the youngster.

"*Open* planned," he said, nodding. "Very *open* planned."

"'Open planned'? What do you mean, 'open planned'? This place is the pinnacle of clutter, a cleaner's nightmare."

The red-faced woman stopped as the file cabinets sprang into action.

Chapter Twenty-Eight

FILE CABINETS

"There is only so much power a file cabinet can hold."—A footman's diary

Mr Ex, scrunched against a wall, was feeling his age. A filing cabinet had him pinned like a dead moth; it was as dignified as a bowel examination and just as painful.

He stared at the grey metal pressed against his face. He'd been hoping for a mere drawer opening, not an onslaught of metallic tombstones hell-bent on crushing; one move had them jostling like watchdogs.

"This is your idea of a good idea," Legless hissed through his teeth.

"Forgot the cabinets were indiscriminate," muttered Mr Ex.

"And we're tied to chairs," said Legless.

"You're still tied to a chair?"

"Yes—aren't you?"

Mr Ex squinted down at the remains of his chair and said nothing. His chair had crushed like a matchstick and now lay about his feet like confetti, apart from an annoying piece sticking into the small of his back.

He tried to ease into a more comfortable position; the file cabinet pressed closer.

"Those women must have tampered with things," he said.

"You reckon?" said Legless.

"How was I to know?" said Mr Ex.

"You should have left things to me. I had that youngster eating out of my hands."

"Eating? She was tying them up," snapped Mr Ex.

"Very funny," mumbled Legless.

"Lycra can only take you so far," said Mr Ex.

Legless sighed.

"You took it too far. Sculpting was *my* big mistake," said Mr Ex.

Here we go, thought Legless.

"Gave you a big head, started off all that strutting of yours."

"I don't strut," snapped Legless.

"Give a man a sock and suddenly he's a god," said Mr Ex.

"The sock was your idea," said Legless.

"You had a drawerful down there."

"I was merely surviving," said Legless.

"Pfff—is that what you call it?" grunted Mr Ex.

"If parading my wares gets us a bit of freedom, then yes, I'd call it surviving; might have worked if you hadn't shouted that damnable word."

Mr Ex said nothing. What a fool he had been to believe in love.

Legless was as interested in him as the Guru was in tracksuit pants; in fact, he and Legless were as likely to get it on as the Guru was of wearing a pair.

"I've brought the lubricant!" yelled the youngster from the door.

"Good girl. Now warm it with your hands," said Legless.

She looked at the sea of papers strewn across the floor, the cabinets menacingly jostling, and the Lycra-torn calf of Legless. She stopped at the dark liquid coagulated about the top of the tube.

"Don't think so. It will stain."

"Staining? I'm strapped against a wall like the skin of a four-legged creature with last year's tax files up my arse and you're talking of staining?"

"It's a bugger to get out," she interrupted.

"Just send the tube this way," snapped Legless.

"You're near the window—do you think it's a good idea?" said Mr Ex.

"Perhaps you'd better skid it across the floor then."

"What?" said the youngster with a hurl of the tube. It sailed through the air and out the window.

"Shit," muttered the men.

"No worries, there are plenty more," she said, disappearing, deaf to the men's "don't go . . ."

She could not wait to get away.

Legless, when cornered, was not so lovable . . .

Escaping the cabinets had been easy for the street women. They took one look at the cabinets pressing forward like Dr Who Daleks and headed for the hills.

Apart from the youngster.

She, finishing a firm knot about Legless's torso, faltered.

Legless wiggled his hands free and began tossing anything he could grab. Cups, pencils, and paper flew at the cabinets with as much effect as confetti until Legless, cornered like a wildcat and swearing like a wrestler, reached into his Lycra . . . balls of socks flew through the air like useless missiles.

The youngster darted for the door.

"Come back, you damnable wench," he yelled with a crazed look.

Beryl, pushing the ex-leader like he was a bin on wheels, was halfway down the corridor when the three women appeared and ran toward her.

"Those things are alive," said the red-faced woman.

"Things?" said Beryl.

"The storage units."

"Oh, those. Did you get a nice cup of caffeine?" said Beryl, attempting a bit of humor.

"Caffeine?" snapped the red-faced woman. "There are cups and saucers all over the place."

"Not to mention the files—skidded three times," said String Bean.

"Whatever they are, they're alive and mashing. The men are squashed against the walls like last night's potatoes."

"You treacherous hussies," yelled Legless.

"Bit noisy for a potato," said Beryl, enjoying her newfound banter.

"God knows how long they've got," said the red-faced woman. "How are we to get them out?"

"Do we have to?" muttered the youngster.

Beryl glanced at the ball of socks by the doorway. The mystery of Legless had vanished with a thrust of underwear.

"We haven't time for that," she said. "We've a planet to save."

The red-faced woman and String Bean stared at her.

"You want us to leave them?"

"That Legless is as slippery as an enema. He'll find a way out."

"Too right," muttered the youngster.

"You should be ashamed of yourself," said Manifesto the Great.

Beryl threw him a glare. "No man does a spot of entrapment and gets away with it—not on my watch."

"Can they even breathe?" said the red-faced woman.

"Come back, you four-legged suffragettes," yelled Legless.

"They can breathe," muttered Beryl.

"But ma'am," pleaded String Bean. "Can we not at least make sure they are watered and toileted?"

Beryl pulled a face.

"We are, after all, civilized."

"You treacherous hussies," yelled Legless.

"At least watered," muttered the red-faced woman.

Beryl sighed.

"Very well." She turned to the youngster. "You can water, but don't listen . . ."

The youngster looked down the passage to see a mug crash to the floor, followed by a "you hideous banshees."

"Me? Why Me?"

"She's not coming back, is she?" said Mr Ex.

"She could be."

"Hardly—you called her a harlot," said Mr Ex.

"I didn't mean her specifically."

Legless, with a gasp, cocked his head; Mr Ex was on the other side of the window.

"There is another option."

"I know what you're thinking."

"What else can we do?"

"No."

"It is our only hope."

"There is no hope on a window ledge," said Mr Ex.

"We have no choice," said Legless.

"But you're wearing sandals—you'll skid. And that Lycra of yours is no match for the wind."

"I wasn't talking of me."

"Oh?" said Mr Ex.

"You think I don't know what happened to your chair?" said Legless.

"Shit," mumbled Mr Ex.

Chapter Twenty-Nine

TROLLEYS

"The pushing of a trolley requires balance, precision, and a one-pound coin."–Operator One

*B*ette was starting to feel her old self again.

She had just witnessed the tossing of lubricant on screen one, and while the others were laughing, she was thinking.

Where was Beryl?

She turned to screen two. Catching sight of a familiar face pushing a cleaning trolley with purpose, she stopped.

"Is that what's-her-face?"

"She's in charge of trolley hygiene," said Operator Two.

"Cleaning cleaner trolleys?" said Bette.

"Wheel squeaking. She has a roomful, she'll be in there for hours."

Bette nodded.

Wheel-squeaking duty was the lowest of the low; it involved dirty hands, rubbish tools, smelly oil, and a dark room with no window.

Just perfect for the likes of Hilda.

Beryl watched as Hilda disappeared around the corner. She almost smiled. *This is a job for Beryl.*

❖

Beryl stood in the passageway, her hands firmly gripping the ex-leader's wheelchair, pondering her next move.

"So what're you gonna do now?" jeered Manifesto the Great.

"Shut it," snapped Beryl.

"Told you, leadership is all about planning."

"You did not."

"Did too."

"You talk in riddles, and your advice is as much good as that appendage of yours."

"At least I have an appendage."

"Pfff—who'd want one of those?" said Beryl.

The youngster, running past, stopped.

"Say what you like," said Manifesto the Great, "you can't do much without planning."

"What are we to do with him?" said String Bean.

The youngster thought about the lubricant. "I know a place."

"What about the gym?" said the red-faced woman.

"It's the first place they'll look," said Beryl.

"A room where no one goes," said the youngster. "Where all the lubricant is kept."

The women pulled a face.

"For wheels and things," she snapped.

"Pfff," said the ex-leader.

"Trolley wheels," said the youngster. "It's down a few floors . . ."

The woman watched as the youngster slung the ex-leader over her shoulder with hardly a grunt.

"See here—what are you playing at?" snapped the ex-leader.

"Well, come on," said the youngster. She turned to Beryl. "It's a totally incognito place."

It took minutes for the women to arrive—minutes of downstairs running with a hand clapped over the ex-leader's mouth, the wheelchair under an arm, and very little puffing.

In fact, the only one out of breath was the ex-leader. A hand covering one's mouth while shouting "see here!" can do that to an old man.

They stopped at the door marked *Trolley Hygiene*.

Beryl pushed the door open.

"I'm still a leader . . ." yelled the ex-leader.

The red-faced woman shoved the wheelchair in.

The youngster followed, flopping Manifesto the Great onto his chair like a pile of wet laundry.

He cursed.

The door slammed shut.

"Oi----You can't leave me here!" he shouted.

The youngster appeared, handed him a drink, and shut it again.

He heard the click of a lock, banged the door, then stopped. He looked at his iced water and sipped.

It had been a long time since he'd tasted water like that . . . he closed his eyes, almost enjoying the taste, then took another sip.

His eyes adjusted to the dark as he looked around.

He had no idea there were so many trolleys.

Chapter Thirty

THE SPARK PLUG

"No one thought of what would happen when the men were too old to move, let alone if they went on strike."–Manifesto the Great

Hilda was fifteen when lust overtook her. Now at the same age, Knee-High too had a lust, not for appendages, but for something better.

She, a streetwise chancer, had made the most of being ignored, perfecting the art of being unseen.

She learned things she wasn't supposed to, mainly that those in power talked through their backside and the minions had no idea.

Years of "short" jokes spurred her on.

She ducked and dove, skidded and swerved, bolting between the escaping men like there was no tomorrow. Knee-High ran like there was a fire behind her and a lake in front, determined to get away from "those bastards in the city."

Hilda headed around the corner and broke into a sprint.

Vegas, waiting, joined her.

"They bought it. Let's go," said Hilda.

They raced to the Trolley Hygiene room, unlocked the door, and pushed it open with the trolley. The trolley knocked Manifesto the Great to the back of the room.

He jolted awake.

"Oi! Whose that?"

Hilda slammed the door shut.

"What was that?" said Vegas.

"Let me out."

The women stopped.

"Is that the ex-Leader?" whispered Vegas.

"Ex pickling nothing—get me out of here."

Hilda creaked the door open a crack. She peered into the shadows, catching sight of the ex-leader, glass in hand, glaring at her.

Hilda, a woman of ingenuity, saw an opening . . .

"Get me some meat," she said.

"Meat? Are you crazy? That stuff is as illegal as a man's jockstrap."

"Pseudo, the good stuff."

"It's too late for meat," said the ex-leader.

Vegas looked at Hilda.

"I'm done for."

"Hardly. There's still a bit of life in the old boy yet," said Vegas with a tentative slap.

"Don't you call me old," hissed Manifesto the Great.

❖

The Operators stared at screen four.

Mex had the Guru by the throat as they fell off the cliff of the quarry and cascaded down.

The third man picked up the loincloth that had caught on the ledge.

❖

Mr Ex slid his foot from the cabinet and made for the ledge.

He twisted his face to look out the window; it was a few stories down. If he fell, he might survive—others had.

A cabinet grunted, rumbled, and toppled.

"What was that?" said Legless.

Another cabinet tumbled.

Legless turned to see files spilling onto the floor.

Mr Ex put his foot on the ledge.

Well, it's been a good life, he thought, *all things considered. Might have been nice to do a few more statues. Perhaps one of the Guru—that would have really pushed his talents.*

Legless head-butted the cabinet in front of him. It toppled like a domino, crashing into another, sparking a chain reaction of tumbling.

As the last one clattered to the ground, Legless stared ahead at Mr Ex's sandals poised on the window ledge . . .

"Shit."

Out on the ledge, the wind rustling through his nether regions, Mr Ex shivered, his eyes fixed on the emporium opposite. The street was a long way down, and he figured if he didn't look at it, it wasn't there.

Mr Ex had never noticed Planet Hy Man's first emporium before, a bog-standard affair named after the great Wife-ie herself.

Wife-ie's Beaut Emporium was looking a trifle rundown. In fact, many had talked of demolition, and as he stared at the *Wife-ie's Beaut Emporium* with all its *E*s missing, he saw the merit in such a plan. Until, that is, he noticed the large, dark windows filling with faces staring at him: the checkout chicks of the emporium.

"Why am I here again?" he shouted. "'Cause if it's to escape incognito, I think we're buggered."

"The cabinets are done for," said Legless.

"What?"

"I said you can come back inside."

"Come? What do you mean come?"

"Back," yelled Legless, "inside."

"My insides? Speak up, I can't hear you over this wind."

"Change of plan, the cabinets have conked out."

"Conked? Must you talk in riddles?" said Mr Ex. "I have an audience here, and it's a little off-putting."

The faces across from him waved a "no need to jump" wave.

He attempted an "I'm not jumping, just getting a bit of fresh air" wave back, skidded, and stopped.

The faces gasped.

"I said the cabinets have run down. Different plan."

"Run? On a ledge? Do you hate me that much?"

"Just come back inside."

"Inside? Which window?"

"This window."

Legless poked his head out. "Give me your hand."

"Oh, god of galaxies, I thought you'd never ask."

Vegas, grumbling along the corridor, was trying to "think on her feet"—a saying Hilda was fond of.

The Building of Opulence was in disarray.

Women sporting birds-nest hair wandered the corridors looking disorientated, some trying light switches, others yelling, "They're buggered!"

The calm had gone, and in the midst of such confusion, Vegas wondered . . . if taking care of the ex-leader had been such a good idea.

He was, after all, a man.

She, on the search for food "befitting a leader"—as Hilda put it—along with perhaps "some caffeine," headed up stairs.

The corridor was in the sort of shambles that would make the fingers of any cleaner itch to clean. The walls and floor were lined with wheelchair skid marks from the ex-leader's chair. Socks, mugs, and stationary were piled outside the room with a view. And in the midst of it all was a male voice shouting with the sort to urgency that had a decent woman like Vegas racing to help.

"Just take my hand, will you?"

She headed into the room with a view, skating across the highly polished floor on an open file. Stopping with a robust clatter into an upturned file cabinet, she looked up to see a shaky Legless balancing with one foot on an upturned cabinet, his other on the window ledge —like he was going to jump.

"Don't do it," she shouted.

He jolted, sending Mr Ex's sandals flying. The file cabinet toppled; Legless followed, landing with a "shit!"

He stared at the bottom of the file cabinet, inches from his face.

A trapdoor fell open, cutting the side of his nose, and before he had time to rub a small spark plug rolled out.

"Are you still there?" yelled Mr Ex.

Vegas raced to the window ledge, while Legless slid the spark plug into his pocket.

"Just coming," he said as he fingered the metallic mechanism.

Chapter Thirty-One

THE SANDAL

"There is nothing more frustrating than getting what you want and realizing you don't want it anymore."–Bette

Bette, fine-tuning her plan to put Beryl at the heart of Trolley Hygiene, was pondering what to do with that what's-her-face cleaner when she caught sight of the sort of dust that would annoy any cleaner "worth their salt."

She ran her fingers along the trail of dust.

The Operators moved to stop her and probably would have if the falling of file cabinets had not reverberated through the building.

As the paper-thin walls shook, books tumbled . . . leaving the *Wifeie's Emporium* catalog strangely solitary.

Bette, her hand poised by the catalog, stopped.

"What this?"

"Nothing!" shouted the Operators.

Mr Ex's sandal flashed past the window.

Beryl and her entourage were heading away from the Trolley Hygiene room when they heard the plopping of the file cabinets and following reverberations.

Beryl stopped.

"What was that?" she hissed.

"It sounded like a plopping of sorts," said the red-faced woman.

"Plopping—what is a plopping?"

"Sort of like flopping but with heavier objects," said the youngster, who was proving to be smarter than first thought.

The woman looked at her.

She shrugged. "Something like a cabinet."

"Shhhh," said String Bean. She gestured to the operation room.

They stopped just outside it.

Beryl peered in, catching sight of the bookcase trapdoor wide open and Bette, duster in hand, disappearing into the dark tunnel. A tunnel Beryl knew like the back of her hand.

The door closed behind Bette.

"Shit," said Kate.

"Perhaps not," said Beryl, entering like she owned the place.

Kate blinked.

"Our leader has lost some of the plot."

"Well, yes, but . . ."

"Maybe a bit of 'me time'?" Beryl looked about the room.

"In there?" said an Operator. "With a duster?"

"Sometimes a leader needs a spot of cleaning to reboot the thought process."

Kate nodded. She wasn't sure if she agreed, but she liked the way Beryl put it.

Bette, picking her way through paper cups, hemp stubs, and galaxy-knows-what-else in the passageway, didn't hear a thing.

Thanks to an ingenious sunlight-reflecting roof it was anything but dark, Bette could see everything. She could hardly walk for rubbish; she skidded on a tough bit of crust and stopped.

"This place is in shambles," she yelled.

No one answered. The images on the screens were blurring, fuzzing, draining the last of any power.

She looked about the mess mumbling to herself.

What she wouldn't have given for just a little enthusiasm from her girls.

She picked a rock-hard biscuit and nibbled around the edges.

One of Kate's precious biscuits, tossed aside like a used tissue.

She tutted.

Many a worker would give a day's wage for one of these.

Then she remembered how much some were paid and felt ashamed.

Where was her brave new world, her equality? When did they start resting on their laurels?

She tossed the offending biscuit into a bag, followed by a crust and a few stubs, then stopped at a pile of rat's dropping.

It was so old it crumbled in her hands.

"This place is so disgusting even the rats don't come here anymore," she shouted, and when no one answered, she continued to clean.

The checkout chicks from Wife-ie's Emporium had quickly rallied, collecting anything for a "soft landing." Within minutes, they appeared on the streets pushing wheelie bins full of rubbish and laundry.

They lined up the bins, ready to catch, and looked up at the ledge.

They had never seen a man on a ledge before, especially one so old and rickety. They wanted to do something, stop the "poor old bugger" from splattering on the pavement.

They stared at his twisted, arthritic legs.

"Look at him shivering like a leaf."

"What would send him up there like that?"

"Probably as mad as a turtle."

"An addict, more like it," muttered a cynic.

The others looked at her.

"Should be put out to graze with the four-legged creatures—well past it."

They stopped.

"What are you saying? We should let him splatter to his maker?"

"Well, no—I'm here aren't I, ready to catch? Just saying," said the cynic, she stopped gestured to the ledge.

Legless peered onto the ledge, stretched out his hand . . .

Mr Ex made to grab and skidded on his remaining sandal, sending it hurling to the ground . . .

The women gasped . . .

Mr Ex stumbled, his fingers flashing past Legless's hands . . .

"Nooooo . . .

Chapter Thirty-Two

KNEE-HIGH

"The movement of a turtle can take many by surprise."—Mex

The quarry, set in a large field away from everywhere, was huge, so huge that the men heading for the outlands on one side could not be seen by the Guru or Mex on the other.

Beryl, however, had a birds'-eye view of the Operator's screen before the power died. In fact, it was one of the last things she saw. Apart, that is, from Verruca.

❖

Knee-High stared down at her portable intercom-thingy strapped to her wrist. She had ten minutes, *max*. She, like all good Operators, knew the screens were on their last legs, and without a screen, this portable intercom-thingy was merely a bad piece of jewelry.

Soon she would be as incognito as an ant.

Kate did argue the merits of handing out a portable intercom-thingy to the likes of Knee-High, but as Bette put it, "If it's good enough for Beryl, it's good enough for a trolley pusher."

Catching Knee-High's affronted look, Bette patted her head.

"It's Knee-High," snapped Knee-High.

Not the best start to a "saving the planet" mission, but then Knee-High had no intention of saving the planet. She knew different.

Knee-High was heading for the hippie colony, a place where people like her had a better life: a life away from the *"poor cow"* looks of her comrades.

By the time Knee-High arrived at the quarry, the young man was staring motionlessly over the ledge of the quarry with the lookout turtle growling at his heels.

Knee-High hid behind the only tree for miles.

She could hear the Guru yelling like he was thrashing the living daylights out of someone.

She peered from behind the tree . . .

Scrabbling about the relics of robots was a muscular teenager rattling a skeleton of an old man by the neck, his feet air-running like a crazed cartoon character.

She stared closer. He didn't have a stitch on . . . and she could see everything, including his dangly bits jiggling like a bag of marbles.

She gulped.

Knee-High was not the sort to panic, but recognizing that power-house of a teenager set her pulse racing like a drumroll.

What the galaxy was that Mex doing here?

"Take that!" yelled the Guru with a useless punch.

Mex didn't move; his swing was as wide as a barn door.

"And that!" he yelled.

Mex smiled.

The turtle army, with mechanical chuckles, pulled out their rollups. *This* was better than rugby.

"I'll have you for dinner!" screeched the Guru. "Mashed into my peas and carrots!"

Mex's laugh echoed across the quarry, jolting the lookout turtle into action.

He sunk his teeth into the young man's calf.

The young man jumped with a squeal.

Mex looked up to see the young man waving a pair of trousers at the turtle . . .

The Guru took a swipe.

She waved his fist away as if it were a fly, her eyes on the young man now racing toward the tree with the lookout turtle nipping at his heels.

The young man scaled the tree.

The turtle circled the trunk.

"I'll give you what for," yelled the Guru.

The turtle, baring his teeth, reared up, snorted, and turned . . . computing an *incomer*.

Catching sight of the tip of Knee-High's finger pressed against the trunk, it sniffed, switched to spy mode, then tiptoed closer . . .

Knee-High saw the flash of its teeth first.

She scrambled to climb.

The turtle cut her off, circling her like a guard dog.

"Shoo!" hissed Knee-High.

"Incoming! Incoming!" boomed the turtle.

Mex dropped the Guru like a pair of old socks. *Incoming?*

As Mr Ex sailed to the ground, the checkout chicks moved into action, lining up their bins to catch.

"This way."

"No, this way . . ."

They shuffled and dodged, until a motherly woman with a speed that surprised many caught Mr Ex with her legendary "lunge and push."

A move perfected from years of catching laundry from a shoot that spewed out sheets faster than projectile vomit.

Mr Ex landed on a pile of linen with a soft plop.

The linen was so soft you couldn't smear mascara with it and so high it cushioned his fall like the wrapping of a mother's arms.

The fresh smell of ocean air hit him.

He didn't move.

The motherly one tapped his shoulder.

"Sir?"

He said nothing, feigning sleep. He wanted to lie there forever inhaling this wonderful scent, forgetting the last few days. *Legless and those dastardly filing cabinets.*

"Sir!"

He sighed.

The cynic pushed the motherly one out the way with a "here, let me." "*You okay?*" she bellowed into his ear.

Mr Ex peered up at the checkout chicks.

He had never been to the emporium, let alone seen a dolled-up checkout chick before.

He eyed their fifties perms and red lips.

Had he died and gone to Earth?

"Am I dead?" he muttered.

They chuckled.

"Is this New York?"

"No, honey, you're dazed," said the motherly one.

They wheeled him into the cafeteria, then tilted a glass of bubbly water to his lips as the massage therapist inspected his limbs.

Catching sight of bruising, she tutted.

"Cycling abuse. I have heard of it but never seen it."

"You don't know the half of it," he muttered.

The others nodded.

"This Bette has gone too far," she said.

Bette, engrossed in the sheer magnitude of cleaning the damnable tunnel, was oblivious to everything.

The silence soothed her.

She chose to hear nothing, not even the scream of a falling Mr Ex or the panicky yelling of the check-out chicks.

She didn't want to.

Let them get on with it, she told herself as the bags of rubbish piled up. Until, that is, she heard a male voice.

Was that Jack?

❖

The lookout turtle circled.

Knee-High lobbed a stone at it. If that Mex caught her, she was a goner . . .

The lookout turtle growled.

She scrambled a kick.

The lookout turtle dodged.

"Here," the young man said, stretching out his hand.

She made to reach, then squinted and stopped.

A pillar of muscle blocked her view.

Shit . . .

Mex stared down at the face who took the piss all those years ago and stopped. It was Knee-High, so small she could not only sit on a turtle but lie on it.

For the second time that day, mixed feelings filled Mex, and before she could sort them out, the Guru jumped onto her back with an octopus's wrapping of limbs.

Her eyes locked with Knee-High's as the Guru's dangly bits pressed into the small of her back.

Without even thinking, Mex kicked out, catching the lookout turtle.

It sailed into the air.

The portable intercom-thingy flashed on.

"Catch it," yelled Beryl.

The turtle landed with a *thud*, rolling onto its back near Verruca's feet.

"Pick it up," yelled Beryl.

Verruca grunted. Helping a turtle roll off its back was not as easy as she thought, let alone picking it up.

"Forward," shouted the Captain.

The turtles charged up the hill like a plague of rabbits, knocking Verruca to the ground. The lookout turtle, with not even a backward glance, let alone a thank-you, jumped up with a sprint and followed.

"Get up!" shouted Beryl.

Verruca, flat on her back with a mechanical appendage in a way-too-personal place, fumed.

She could be at home drinking rubbish caffeine, working away at her dead-end job, collecting, storing, hiding her mother's musings, instead of on her back with a Mae West leg up her arse.

"These things are dying . . . power cut . . . must make the most . . . most . . . most . . . moooost . . ." Beryl's face twisted and blurred.

"Get stuffed," Verruca yelled, followed by a hurl of the dying portable intercom-thingy, which crashed against the torso of a turtle robot.

The screen cracked, splitting Beryl's face into thousands of pieces.

Chapter Thirty-Three

KNEE-DEEP

"A quarry is just a posh name for a dump."–Mex

Beryl and Kate stared at the blank screen, well aware that the portable intercom-thingy had been hurled.

"Does that burst into fire too?" said Operator One.

Kate sighed. "Probably."

"Oh—and Knee-High's?"

Kate nodded, avoiding the glare of the Operators.

"It seemed like a good idea at the time," she muttered.

"She's so small; how much of a flame would it take?" said Operator One.

Operator Two turned to Beryl. "Do you think she'll be all right?"

"I don't know," said Beryl. "The last thing I heard was 'get stuffed.'"

Verruca's wrist portable intercom-thingy burst into flames, sparking off a fireball in the quarry.

She ran like a stunt man with the heat of a fire at her heels.

Mex, wrestling with the Guru, stopped.

The Guru, mid boxer stance, gasped.

Knee-High's portable intercom-thingy burst into flames. She screamed manically, tugging at it . . .

Mex flicked it from her wrist, juggled it from hand to hand in a panic . . .

The Guru grabbed and tossed.

The ball of flames landed on a lubricated joint as flammable as hot oil on a gas stove with a bit of hydrogen thrown in.

It exploded, this time igniting the sort of firestorm that would blow a roof off.

"Get down," shouted Mex, pulling the Guru and Knee-High with her.

The turtle army, mid marching, sailed into the air, lifted by a force so strong they twirled like windmills.

Verruca, still running, followed. Hurled into the air, she clutched the Captain, closed her eyes and swore. If she survived, *that damnable Beryl would pay and pay and pickling pay . . .*

"Fall in line . . ." yelled the Captain into the wind, *like anyone could hear.*

❖

Tired, panting, and a decent distance from the quarry, the escaping men were walking, talking of what lay ahead in the outlands.

Then . . .

BOOM!

They stopped.

BOOM!

They stared, openmouthed, as a mushroom-shaped cloud of smoke rose from the quarry, the noise drowning out their gasps.

❖

The smoke cleared.

Mex sat up.

The Guru and Knee-High followed.

They stared in silence . . . the ground was still. Not a chirp of a bird or rustle of a leaf.

The trousers, ripped and blackened, dropped onto the Guru's face. Peeling it off, he looked up at the tree; there was not a leaf—or the young man—on it.

Sliding on his trousers, he stared at the black hole that once housed his beloved Mae West appendages . . .

Not one had survived. Not a turtle shell could be seen. The quarry was now a black hole smoldering in the wind with only one manicured Mae West hand, its middle finger pointing in an "up yours'" gesture.

He stared at the red nail glistening in the afternoon sun.

"Wonder what happened to the young man," said Knee-High.

"And my turtles," said Mex.

The Guru, thinking on his feet, jumped in he had no idea where they were going but damn if he wasn't going to take a chance. "They'll be heading for the hippie colony," he lied. "It's every turtle's dream."

Knee-High, also thinking on her feet, nodded. "Oh, definitely I heard that too."

Mex paused, looked into the distance. They waited for an answer . . .

"This sort of thing calls for a whip," she finally announced.

The Gurus and Knee-High nodded with no idea what she was talking of.

The blast was felt in the operations room, a sort of juddering that could not be passed off as a plopping of cabinets. A sort of juddering that shook the streets, the cups on the table, and any books left on the bookcase.

Kate looked at Beryl. "Shit."

Beryl said nothing. Instead, she took in the frantic, guilt-ridden look of Kate and, with a "you weren't to know" pat, thought—*That's another rival down.*

Beryl's ambitions were getting closer.

The *BOOM!* blasted down the main street.

The *M* from the Wife-ie's Emporium sign plopped to the ground.

The checkout chicks gasped.

Women ran to the windows; others stopped in the streets.

The main street had been built of solid stuff—back in the days when workers were hell-bent on making a decent town to live in—yet it juddered like a plate of jelly.

Mr Ex said little.

The massage therapist was working on his big toe, and he didn't want her to stop.

❖

At first, Verruca was a speck on the horizon they hardly noticed until a turtle snorted.

The men looked up; in the distance was a fleet of flying turtles with Verruca and the young man grimly hanging on.

The men gasped.

The turtles they remembered were large garden destroyers. These things were tinier than rats with flying appendages on par with an Earth helicopter.

The turtles, it seemed, were excellent flyers, a gift they had no idea of until being propelled into the air sparked the rising of rotating blades.

It took them by surprise, but once they got used to it, it felt as natural as, well, poking a tongue.

"Fall in line!" yelled the Captain for the hundredth time.

"We heard you the first time!" yelled the lookout turtle, which sent him into an off-balance spin.

Verruca, clutching on for dear life, swore. "Don't talk!" she shouted.

"What?" he shouted, setting off another spin.

"Wait until we land," yelled Verruca, now upside down and feeling sick.

"Land?" the lookout turtle yelled. "We're heading for the hippie colony. The Captain has always dreamed of going there." He gulped. He was feeling pretty sick as well.

The men looked at each other.

"Follow those turtles," shouted one.

As Mr Ex was wheeled away, Legless watched, twisting the spark plug in his hand.

A storage system—who'd have thought?

He smiled.

This will be the making of me.

Vegas, catching Legless's smile, stopped. "You weren't going to jump, were you?"

"Me? As if."

She stared at his hand. "Was there something in that file cabinet?"

"No . . ."

"Oh." She eyed him suspiciously. "You sure?"

"Of course I'm sure. Do I look like I'm lying?"

"Well, yes, you do."

"That's just the way I'm standing."

"Hmmm," she muttered, unconvinced. "You lot lie like there's no tomorrow."

"Us lot?"

"Yes, you—*men.*"

"I am a mere cyclist trying to sort the energy crisis . . ." He smiled.

She threw him a glare.

" . . . and save my pal."

Vegas was hardly convinced. In fact, she was confused, disorientated, and not quite sure what to do next. Helplessly watching an old man almost die can do that to someone, especially someone with a soft heart like Vegas.

Legless, watching her confusion, took a chance. "so what are you here for?" he eyed her apron. "Not to save the energy crisis."

"Well no."

"Or a Pal?

"I...."

"So why are you here?"

She gulped thinking of the ex leader and Hilda.

"Ummmm..." she blushed, looked about the mess, spied a plate of Kate's biscuits untouched by the mayhem and thought on her feet.

"Biscuits," she said "There is bugger all left at our beverage hub."

Chapter Thirty-Four

THE SAILING OF SOCKS

"Beware of a woman with stiff hair. It usually means she's spent too long looking at herself to think of others."–Fanny

Beryl, still in the operations room, was trying to think and not getting anywhere.

The bigwigs were arguing, the Voted Ins were telling them to "shut it," and Kate was waffling on about lighting up the city with "a good old-fashioned Victorian lamp."

Bigwig One snorted.

"What the sperm is the difference between a Victorian lamp and what we have?"

"Oil," said Kate.

"That stuff?" said a voice from the back.

"Or is it gas?" muttered Kate.

"You're having a laugh," snapped the market cleaner.

"Well, no . . . I was thinking of redesigning."

"That stuff is as combustible as an egg box. In fact, it makes an egg box fire look like a puff of smoke, a mere fart in the world of explosions. Why not built an Earth socket and stick a knife into it?"

"Don't be stupid," said Kate.

"Hurl some water at it."

"Very funny . . ." snapped Kate.

"Throw a bit of hydrogen in, split an atom."

"All right, I get your point," growled Kate.

"Get a good old mushroom effect," said the market cleaner.

"I was only trying to help," screeched Kate.

The market cleaner stopped.

Kate looked about the blank faces. "I don't see any of you coming up with anything."

"Well, we didn't make explosive watches," said the voice from the back.

Kate turned to the voice. "They are not watches."

"Still exploded," muttered Bigwig One.

"You try sitting all day with that knee-grabbing ex-leader."

Beryl sighed, and before she could shout "enough!" an arm had dragged her from the room.

"Come with me," whispered a male voice into her neck.

Beryl, surprised at such a delicious sensation, said nothing, allowing herself to be whisked into the nearest broom closet.

She stared into the dark.

Legless made to flick on his portable intercom-thingy.

"Don't," she shouted.

He laughed. "It's disconnected," he said, adjusting the angle of the light so it showed his best side.

"We men are not completely stupid." His lips closed in on her neck. "I have what you are looking for."

She thought of his socks. "Not just now."

He grabbed her hand.

"Really, I have a city to save," said Beryl.

He slid the spark plug into her palm. "

The secret is storage," he said. "And a few false promises . . ."

That night, the last of Legless's socks went sailing out the window, landing on an unsuspecting passerby.

It took minutes for Beryl to discover there was more to a dangling bit than just dangling . . . and seconds for Legless discover there was more to Beryl than stiff hair.

Beryl was insatiable, and a sock was the least of it. In fact, with a mere flick of a forefinger, her hair melted, like the rest of her, into a gooey mush of "oooh, more please."

Good old-fashioned procreation, she discovered, was not merely for . . . well, procreation.

Pleasing Beryl was better than expected; in fact, it was so much fun that Legless wore himself out, dispensing more seed than a gardener in springtime.

So prolific was he that he was soon dozing—snoozing the blissful sleep of a man waiting for his dispenser to fill.

And while he was out for the count, Beryl was teasing her hair back into place with a new edge.

An edge to sort, stride, boss, dominate, and leave Bette humming in the passageway with a year's supply of dusters. Beryl felt like a million dollars; she had the magic solution and a very happy landing pad.

Soon she was entering meetings with a certain glow and her beehive askew . Not that anyone would mention it; Beryl ruled with a look as hard as her beehive.

After one orgasm, she promised Legless a mention; after several, she promised him a portrait in the hall of greatness.

"I want more than that," he said, tracing the line of her nipple.

"Darling," she said, "if you use that brain of yours half as well as your appendage, there'll be way more than a mention. You'll be at the leader's table, beside me."

Legless looked into her eyes and believed every word. *His appendage was amazing.*

A few days later, Verruca walked into the hippie centre a blackened, angry woman. Behind her, were a few hungry looking men, a motley crew of limping turtles, and the young man perched on the Captain's back telling her to "barge in and don't bother knocking."

Turns out landing, for a turtle, is not as easy as flying . . .

Mex leathered up and, with her whip by her side, headed out into the outland. She had been given the task of bringing back men, a task she relished.

There had been gossip of fieldworkers fearlessly ripping men limb from limb—men who whimpered at the drop of *whatever*.

She knew it was all a load of bollocks spread by the powers that be to keep the minions, well, minions. Besides, she had her turtles to retrieve.

Knee-High and the Guru followed . . .

The hippie colony was not what they expected. It was hardly a colony; more a cluster of sheds, tree houses, and way too many young-sters kicking about in the baking sun.

Under the tree houses, in the only shade for miles, lounged the escaped men and turtle robots clutching hemp roll-ups of various lengths.

"We're testers," chuckled the lookout turtle.

"Yeah!" yelled another.

"And it's hard work," said the Captain, wiping his brow.

The Guru blinked, looking out at the parched feilds. "This place could do with a few verandas," he said, "and a cooling device."

"Perhaps a windmill?" said Knee-High.

"You'd need an army for that," muttered Mex, a comment the turtles and the men chose to ignore.

Mr Ex spent days under the massage therapist's hands and then, because he was such a decent chap, offered to return the favor.

She blushed. "You, massage?"

He smiled. "Just your feet," he said. "I can see you stand way too long."

With a quick flick of her shoe, she thrust her right foot his way and was soon moaning with pleasure.

For Mr Ex, working on a woman's foot was like working on a piece of sculpture—without the knife.

His hands had authority, and the massage therapist's bunions were putty in his hands.

It didn't take long for the word to get out. Soon he was massaging feet all day and was so overcome with women he grabbed the first man he saw hiding by the bins outside.

He had escaped from the secret corridor, scurrying from the insane singing of a "cleaner gone mad."

Others followed and soon

Mr Ex had team of men practicing on mechanical rats until they were good enough for a checkout chick's foot.

"The secret is the bunion," he said. "Get that soothed and the rest is a breeze."

Chapter Thirty-Five

POLISHING

"The Fairness Act says one thing and does another."–Kate

A year later

Kate was standing by the tie stall in the market. She was looking for something befitting the new room with a view.

It had just been equipped with a table so large you could do the splits on it and still have room for a cartwheel. Not that Kate had any intention of doing such things , but she knew which side her bread was buttered on, and keeping in with Beryl with a decent tie was one of them.

She pulled a purple tie from the stand; its large flared bottom was just what she was looking for. The Voted In had moved into the room with a view, and their tastes had become more flamboyant: black suits with a splash of color around the neck.

"How much?" she asked.

"It's on the ticket," snapped Bigwig One with a dirty look.

"Oh, I didn't see." Kate feigned a laugh.

She spied the price and stopped.

"If you're looking for a bargain, forget it. Still waiting for those promised biscuits," said Bigwig One.

Kate blushed. "It is the busy season—legislation, lots of signing." She sighed. "You remember."

Bigwig Two pulled the tie from Kate's hand.

Remember—how could she forget?

A year ago she was signing things off; now, thanks to that stuck-up Beryl and her Voted Ins, she was merely a stall owner obeying whatever was so-called "signed off" on.

"Just pickle yourself off," snapped Bigwig Two. "Go back to your bum-crawling."

"But—"

"You heard. There's another tie stall down the alley," said Bigwig One. "They sell that pseudo-Earth snakeskin—more your style."

The bigwigs watched Kate disappear into the crowd with the sort of scowl that could sour milk.

"Turncoat," muttered Bigwig One.

"Arse-licker."

"Snakeskin's too good for her," snapped Bigwig One.

❖

Legless knocked on the door of the Trolley Hygiene room.

Manifesto the Great tossed his rag at the heap in the corner and laughed. "Enter at your peril!"

Manifesto the Great had carved out a career of oiling, which seemed to not only bring out a man of wit but a man with a love for order and shiny wheels.

He spent his time sorting trolleys. He loved the dark, the smell of oil, and the smooth rolling of a lubricated joint. He had found what he truly enjoyed doing; a tool bench was way better than a cocktail bar, oiling way better than drinking, and as for meat?

Sipping a soy-infused smoothie while sorting a wheel was more his kind of soup.

"Give me your broken trolleys, your wobbly wheels," he shouted, "and I will give you something worth pushing."

Working-class women came and went, bringing their squeaky wheels, which they could have fixed themselves in a jiffy, but making him happy by telling him what a wiz he was felt so much better.

Some sat and watched, mustering *ooh*s and *arrrrgh*s; some even asked him questions about the "good ol' days."

He was so happy he even forgot about his legacy, until Legless started his carrying on.

Legless pushed open the door with his back.

"Oh," muttered Manifesto the Great.

Legless sat the tea tray on an upturned trolley.

"Not there," snapped the ex-leader.

Legless, ignoring him, smiled. "I'm moving up in the world."

Manifesto the Great shifted the tray with a grunt. He was never keen on Legless's seduction plan.

"With the most powerful woman in the city," said Legless.

Manifesto the Great said nothing.

"Seriously, I am," said Legless. "She is a woman in love."

"That woman doesn't love," huffed Manifesto the Great. "She was brought up by the Librarian, for galaxy's sake."

"Exactly," puffed Legless.

"She's a tough old boot, heart of ice."

"She's a desert who needs a decent downpour."

"She's a desert that will drain your balls dry and toss you to the quarry."

"I'll replenish her," said Legless, jumping from the opening door.

Hilda appeared with what looked like a trolley that had been jumped on by an elephant and tossed to the crusher.

She pushed inside with a jocular "you trying to convince old Buggerlugs over there that Ms Beehive has a heart?"

"And a very grateful landing pad." Legless smiled.

"A landing pad's happiness never lasts long," said Hilda, jumping from the opening door.

Vegas squeezed inside the cramped room, shunting Legless into a corner without touching him.

She was not the sort who liked that kind of carrying-on, and no amount of "appendage talk" from Hilda could convince her otherwise.

❖

She tossed a bag of wheels at the ex-leader. "He's not talking of landing pads again, is he?"

Legless glared at the trolley, wondering why he ever bothered to visit.

Manifesto the Great opened the bag of wheels with a sniff. "That spark plug will be the end of you."

"End? It's the beginning. I've her right where I want her. Soon your legacy will be intact, old fella."

"Less of the 'old,'" muttered Manifesto the Great.

"I've heard they're working on a sort of communication pad in the hippie colony," said Vegas.

Legless stopped. "What?"

"Yes. Beryl has ordered an investigation."

Legless blushed; he had no idea.

The ex-leader looked at him.

"Looks like the landing pad is keeping you out of the loop yet again."

Vegas followed Hilda out into the corridor, saying nothing. Hilda was doing her angry march.

"How did you know?" Hilda snapped. "I mean, why you and not me?"

Vegas blushed.

Hilda stopped, pushing her face into Vegas's.

"You're in touch with that Knee HIgh, aren't you?"

"It was she who got in touch with me."

Hilda eyed her pal. "I never thought you'd be so devious."

Vegas's face burned. "I was going to tell you."

"Sure you were." said Hilda. She flashed a smile. "I'm impressed."

"What?"

"Yes, we've got every corner covered thanks to you. The ex-leader, the hippie colony, the room with a view. We're closer than we think, just need that Beryl to make a slipup."

Vegas blinked blankly.

"I thought we were just trying to help," said Vegas.

Hilda let out a manic laughed.

Kate, giving up on the new tie idea, headed back to her studio, the box room by the old room with a view.

The room that had taken her weeks to clear.

The room where she and Legless had spent the last year refining the spark plug into an energy system that did away with stationary bikes.

The only gym left was the gym museum, and the only stationary left was with the odd well-off woman who wanted something to look at apart from Earth in the mirror. A young personal stationary cyclist was still considered a sight worth having, and as young men were rarer by the day, a personal cyclist was as impressive as a penthouse. In fact, only those in a penthouse could afford one.

She stared at the benches sporting tools, plans, templates, and communication devices that *sort of* worked.

She felt sad and alone.

While Legless was reaping the benefits of his hard work and living with "the missus," she was, well, forgotten.

The ex-leader, wrapped up with the likes of Hilda and Vegas, had no time for her, claiming she was as useful as a single shoe.

The Bigwigs hated her, claiming she did nothing; they sat back and watched as the Voted In dispensed with the bigwigs.

Did they not understand? She was too busy helping to sort out the energy crisis to, well, save them.

If only she had a pal.

Someone like her to chuckle over formulas with, talk of ideas, a sort of brainstormer who loved to chat.

She stared at the remaining portable intercom-thingy, which was now illegal. She was under orders to destroy it.

She wiped a tear.

She had argued, but no one listened.

"I just need more time to work out how to detach the flammable section," Kate had said.

Those in the room with a view were having none of it.

"If you can't work out how to detach it by now, you never will," said Beryl.

Kate picked up a portable intercom-thingy, turned it over, and pulled out her screwdriver . . .

It flashed.

Knee High appeared on the screen.

Kate fumbled with the sound.

"We need you," said Knee High.

"Me?"

"Here at the hippie colony."

"Whatever for?" muttered Kate.

"You, your tools, and those portable intercom-thingies of yours."

"They are to be destroyed," she said, choking back a tear. "Despite my new template . . ."

"Take as much as you can," said Knee High.

". . . my new names . . ."

"Just collect your things," said Knee High.

". . . and the expanding screen."

"The Captain will meet you at the quarry," said Knee High. A crisp flicking off followed.

Kate stared at the blank screen. All things considered, every option she had was pretty shitty.

Knee High looked up at the Guru. "Once we get her here, we'll be sorted."

"Sorted? Isn't she the one who made everything explode?"

"Well, yes, but . . . she's got all the tools and the templates."

The Guru tutted. "Like that will make a difference."

Chapter Thirty-Six

FANNY'S HIDDEN PASSAGEWAY

"The 'integration scheme' is a

Verruca was standing by the hedge applying a spot of diking to the trunks.

She was on the side where the fieldworkers hid, and they, along with the Captain, were watching.

In one year, Verruca had made herself not only at home in the hippie colony but a force to be reckoned with, mainly due to her banging on about her "integration scheme."

She, like her mother, dreamed of integration rather than segregation. "We're nothing without the fieldworkers," she loved to say, which was usually greeted with silence.

Working on the hedge was one of her integration schemes, which even the turtles had no interest in. She planned a proper stone wall with proper gates and no more of this face-painting, man-scaring malarkey.

The others thought she was nuts.

For a start, drying washing on stone was pointless—left it even messier.

"Stone is far more durable," said Verruca.

"And tougher on the hands," said the spokeswoman.

"Yes, but a rough hand is way more practical," said Verruca.

"You try telling that to the missus," said a voice from the back.

"You have a missus?" said Verruca.

"Of course. It gets lonely at night."

"But not lonely enough to put up with sandpaper hands," added the spokeswoman.

Verruca stopped.

"I never thought about, you know . . . *that*."

"There is more to us fieldworkers than shouting and face-painting," said the voice at the back.

"That's what I say too," said the Captain.

The fieldworkers stared at the Knee High robot's hard shell reflecting the burning sun.

"But you *are* a robot," muttered one.

He huffed. If he had a cube of hemp sugar for every time he heard that, he'd be as high as a mechanical crow.

"Robots have feelings too," he muttered.

The spokeswoman tossed him a cube with a "here, on the house."

The Captain licked it up, chuckling inside—it always worked.

The colony had an endless supply of hemp and soya, which they used for everything, including their latest: hemp sugar. A substance came across by accident and still in the testing phase, mainly on robots, although the turtles had no idea about any of this. They thought the sugar cubes were a reward.

"I'm off," he said.

The women didn't hear.

"Secret mission," he added.

Verruca stared into the expanse of soya and hemp fields waving in the wind.

"You could get lost in there—never found again," she muttered.

"I won't get lost. I'm on a secret mission," said the Captain.

"We know every blade," lied a voice from the back.

"Never lost," lied another.

"Cheers, I'm off to save the colony," said the Captain.

"Give Kate our love," shouted the spokeswoman, giggling at the Captain's dirty look.

The Captain, clutching several cubes of emergency sugar pilfered from the kitchen, headed off to meet Kate.

He cursed the wretched fieldworkers and their so-called sense of humor. Perhaps this Kate would be different.

Verruca had walked into a colony at the cusp of recycling.

Leftover *anything* was for the compost, which, situated near an unfinished don't-hang-about greenhouse, was the reason said greenhouse was unfinished.

It was the great carbuncle of the hippie colony, a carbuncle that none could endure.

It stank like a century-old air-locked fart, loitering under the nose like a loose hair, penetrating even the thickest of masks.

Greenhouse workers never lasted long; most left gagging, never making it through the first day.

The Captain led Kate past the greenhouse, telling her to hold her nose.

She stopped.

"Keep going," said the Captain, "or you'll drown in that effluent smell."

Kate took one look at the steaming pile of effluent and saw tasty herbs, glorious flowers, and trailing fruit vines.

She breathed in the fumes, and while the Captain gagged, she inhaled—*lush, fertile compost.*

"I'm home at last," she muttered.

Mr Ex appeared outside Wife-ie's Emporium, the sign with both its *W* and *E* now firmly in position.

He eyed the footman, an elderly gent patiently waiting for his caffeine break.

"Recruitments are coming," he said with a pat on his shoulder.

The elderly gent sniffed.

Mr Ex was the first of the new footmen, the first to stand at entrances in a brand-new outfit with hot caffeine breaks and a wealth of women asking his opinion on anything.

Not that he had the answers, but he learned to listen, ask questions, and save his opinions for his memoirs.

The "footman" idea came to him one day when he spied a man sheltering in a doorway.

An idea he sold while massaging feet.

"All the best emporiums in New York have them," he said. "They're called doormen."

"Doormen?" The checkout chicks giggled.

"Yes, and they can massage on the side."

The "massage" bit swung it.

Soon he was managing rather than standing, seated at the worker's canteen table and handing out orders like an army general. He even had time to finish his memoirs, which in the end were sold at the front of the store with him signing copies, until Beryl pointed out footmen do not do "signings."

He did do the odd outland visit, but as most had as much interest in reading as he did in cleaning, he didn't stay long. Just enough for a quick cuppa and a chat about sore feet and the best foot rubs.

If there was one thing he knew about, it was foot rubs. In fact, his next best-seller was exactly that: *The Real Truth of a Foot Rub*.

Every well-off woman under the sun bought one, handing it to their newly appointed footmen with a "here."

Mr Ex was soon cursed by other men.

Women assumed that every man knew how to massage, that they all had hands like Mr Ex's.

In fact, a decent foot rub became the new "decent seeing to," as the men had aged and were too knackered for all that other bed-diving malarkey.

Legless visited now and then, but he never heeded Mr Ex's warning. Mr Ex didn't care. He was too busy. He had an army of footmen under his control, including a particular pert man who dressed the emporium windows.

The window dresser and he got on like a house on fire. They spent their time talking of art and designing mannequins—reminding Mr Ex of the good old sculpting days, except this pert man never wore Lycra and only used socks for his feet.

❖

Mex spent the year toing and froing between the city and the hippie colony.

It didn't take her long to give up on the turtles. They, taking up the testing of all things hemp, had as much interest in army maneuvers as she had in test tubes. They loved the hippie colony, whereas she was as board as a teenager without a mobile.

When she received the order to begin herding, she grabbed her mission with gusto.

The first time she returned, she headed straight to the laboratory.

Having a dangly bit poked into the small of your back is not something a woman would forget in a hurry; in fact, Mex couldn't wait to tell the prodigies. She thought they'd wet themselves.

They didn't even look up; they just talked of a mad cleaner terrorizing Fanny's hidden passageway.

Mex, wondering if the mad cleaner was in fact a group of men, strode into the passage, wipes in hand.

Bette was down for the count when Mex found her, clutching a hoover with a large grin.

She had spent her last breath days ago.

Mex, gulping her sadness, lifted Bette over her shoulder.

Beryl was holding court in the room with a view when Mex entered.

The women, mid arguing, stopped.

Beryl ceased her moment, while the others, openmouthed, had no idea what to do.

She took charge.

She could have had Bette's ashes scattered where all the other cleaners were, but she didn't. Beryl chose to pay homage to the cleaner who "rose above her station" by giving her an obelisk in a dark corner of the Courtyard of Greatness with this inscription:

Our Bette
She was the beginning of the end for men
And the end of the beginning for women.

It was a dignified ending for Bette and a defining moment of leadership for Beryl.

It didn't take long for ivy to cover the obelisk, and soon Bette's legacy was as forgotten as Fanny and her heroic fall.

EPILOGUE

*B*eryl stared out of her new penthouse view. It had a patio, a year's supply of chilled sparkly water, and mirrors in each room. Watching Earth was no mere entertainment for Beryl; it was her duty to learn, especially when it came to the leaders and their mistakes.

Legless looked up at her from his bike. He winked; she winked back.

She claimed she had a high-maintenance hairdo that required cycling on par with an Olympic cyclist.

He knew that it was all bollocks, that she liked to watch his butt, and he happily put on a show.

The ex-leader claimed she was just keeping him busy, out of the way. Legless watched her pour a glass of sparkly.

What would he know?

"I heard there is an investigation," he puffed. "Communications pad in the hippie colony."

She spluttered. "You been in that broom closet again?"

"Trolley Hygiene room," he said.

Beryl drained her glass, moved to Legless, and slid her hand down his back. "Just an idea tossed about," she muttered.

"Oh?"

"Yes. I was going to talk to you about it, but I got sidetracked." She slapped his butt.

It wouldn't be long before she would be the ruler, and it wouldn't be long before she, like all rulers, would realize that ruling wasn't all it was cracked up to be. But as she sat there that day a young, hopeful high roller, she knew one thing: as long as she had Legless to come home to, she could face anything.

❖

A few hours later, a sweaty Legless poured himself a chilled sparkly and sipped.

He looked at his butt, his legs, and his face, noticing new wrinkles about the eyes.

She loves me, he told himself, then opened the fridge and pulled out two cold tea bags and slid them onto his eyes.

He didn't hear Beryl get up, and he didn't see her looking at him, but he felt her hands on his thighs.

"Darling," she said, "come back to bed."

She lifted the teabags from his eyes. "We'll grow old together. I don't care about wrinkles."

***

Would you like to read more?
Then check out **Rebel Without Clue** and find out what happens to Beryl and Legless. Join my mailing list to find out when, or follow me on Book Bub, facebook or even Instagram.
But don't race away just yet...
Turn the page for a taste of things to come

"First impressions never last." —Manifesto the Great, Hy Man's
Geographic, last edition

Chapter One

At half past one on a Saturday morning, Mex arrived in Glasgow. With a small bump, she landed in a bus shelter two feet away from Woody, a dwarf, who was peeing in the corner.

Woody stopped, staggered, and, like a sheep on ice, skidded to the floor. His backpack burst open and its contents scattered onto the pavement. He stared up at the vision before him. She towered over him, a giant, Gothic gran squeezed into a leather outfit even Catwoman would think twice about wearing.

Woody was scared, curious, and confused. *Is she on the pull?* He decided to lay off his mother's antidepressants for a while, worried he was hallucinating.

Mex eyed him curiously. He was collapsed in the corner like a garbage bag, wearing a facial expression she had seen many times. She sighed and looked at the contents of his backpack spread out on the ground—a book, a pen, and a packet of Quavers. She picked up the Quavers and, after a good shake followed by a sniff, tossed the packet back on the ground and then lifted the book like it was a specimen jar to be examined.

"You read these?" she said, with no interest in the answer.

Woody gulped and silently watched as Mex slid his prized Terry Pratchett into her breast pocket and pulled out a whip from her side belt.

Oh, Jesus.

The whip cracked itself around his waist and hoisted him up.

Mary Mother of God . . .

The whip twirled him around in the air and dropped him gently onto his feet—away from the piss.

"I'll be good," promised Woody. "I'll go to church."

The whip unwound from his waist and began to hover about Woody's open fly like a rattlesnake ready to pounce.

Saint Christopher Columbus . . .

The tip of the whip hooked itself around the fly lever.

"Oh. Oh. Oooh. Arrrrrh!"

Then it zipped up his fly and, with a playful tap, led Woody from the bus shelter. Woody, confused by mixed sensations of fear and pleasure, stumbled away as Mex flicked the whip back into its holder.

Woody didn't turn back once; he didn't dare. Even when whoever she was began to yell about "latrines" and the like, he didn't turn back. Fear pushed him forward, away from what, he had no idea, but he knew he wasn't hallucinating. No matter how much dope he had had, she was real.

As Woody drew closer to home, he reduced his speed to a walk, and when he saw other people, he stopped, caught his breath, and let his heart slow to a quickstep. *Everything's the same,* he told himself, *everything is okay.*

"Hey, Woody," shouted Ahmad as Woody strode past the steamy windows of the Bangladesh Tandoori. "No pakora tonight?"

Woody didn't hear. He was two doors from home and nothing was going to stop him from getting there—not even an oversized pakora and Ahmad's famous spicy dip. His stomach was churning like a washing machine; in two minutes the battered sausage and chips he had eaten earlier would be on the pavement.

Woody stopped at the front door of his flat and stared at his *knock if you dare* door knocker. His hand strayed to his fly—it was wedged tight, welded like fingers held together with superglue, stuck so fast that he broke a nail trying to pull it open. Woody knew he would never be able to undo it again. He could waste a whole can of WD-40 on his fly and still it wouldn't budge. He sighed; he was going to have to either spend the rest of his life walking around in camouflage trousers or get the scissors out.

How was he going to explain that to his mother?

The Voted In[1] on Planet Hy Man gasped; on-screen, Woody looked even more compact. They couldn't take their eyes off him; it had been a long time since anyone on Planet Hy Man had seen a man of such caliber.

"Let's track him," said Vegas to the Voted Ins. No one argued. Watching Woody would sure make this ridiculous mission worthwhile. It might even add a bit of spice.

The Voted In are a collection of women who spend their days arguing around the extra-large table in the "room with a view"—the room at the top of the Operations building where no one but the elite and some ancient footmen are allowed.

Previously called the "Blue-Rinse Brigade," they're an assortment of women who are sixty-plus and like to think that they run things, that what they say and agree on enables Planet Hy Man to run smoothly. In truth, they do little but annoy Beryl, the leader, and clutter up any decision-making with useless arguments about cushions, pizza toppings, and how tired they are of the black tuxedo uniforms that all Voted Ins wear.

Although how that came to pass as law is anyone's guess.

After the meeting, they gathered in the refreshment area. Vegas counted a full house—always the way when a new batch of illegal brew arrived. It was like Christmas . . .

At the end of the month, coffee, strong and illegal to the masses but enjoyed by the Voted In, arrived, filling the corridors of power with an aroma that had the Voted Ins' noses twitching with excitement. From their office they would poke their noses out, sniffing like it was the first time caffeine had arrived. Sipping the illegal beverage[2] in the lush surroundings of the room with a view made the tedious job of trying to appease the likes of Beryl worth it.

"This Woody," said Vegas, pouring herself a second brew. "It is agreed he is worth the watching?"

"Oh, absolutely," said one. "If we are going to have to watch reruns of this crazy mission, then Woody will make it bearable."

"Oh, and more," said another. "I mean, he has potential, don't you think?"

Vegas whisked her dairy-free milk, wondering what potential they were talking about while the others chuckled around her.

A footman coughed as he stood at the doorway—he was an elderly man dressed in a footman's uniform that hadn't changed since the post began. It was tight and shiny; in fact, it was so tight that bending to tie a shoelace was done in private, just in case any ripping occurred. It was designed when watching BBC period dramas was all the rage to match the opulent room with a view—a room with an excessive amount of chandeliers and decor that made the Brighton Pavilion look like a bog-standard B&B. All had agreed that a footman poised for action like a poor man's Napoleon Bonaparte would complement the décor.

Of course, everyone forgot that he would age, forgot that the last generation of men, made useless by technology, would shrivel like a balloon in the back of a car once their talents for procreating, story-telling, and wrestling were no longer "required."

The footman coughed again as he began to clear the table.

"Ma'am," he said to Vegas, "is it not time for your foot rub?"

Book 1 ***Rebel Without a Clue*** is out now at your favourite store....

---

1. *Planet Hy Man's politicians. A contradiction in terms as they were never voted in. In the past, they were also known as the "Blue-Rinse Brigade," when they were young enough for hair dye to make a difference.*

2. *Caffeine for the masses is as illegal as bootlegging was on Earth. Keeping the masses alert is greatly discouraged by those in charge; weak decaffeinated tea is all they are allowed.*

The Legacy Of Manifesto The Great

First edition. November 30th, 2021.
Copyright © 2021 Kerrie Noor.
Written by Kerrie Noor.

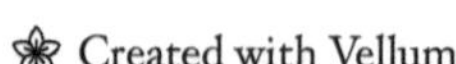 Created with Vellum